Rare Coins
A Collection of Short Stories

Cheryl King

Jacket design, photo/art by Harland King

ISBN: 978-1-7340-3200-0

CONTENTS

DOUBLE DARE

It was a brilliant October morning. The two boys stood at the crest of the steep hill, straddling their bikes. The early October day was unseasonably warm, close to eighty already at ten o'clock in the morning; the air heavy with humidity and perfectly still...not a breath of a breeze. "You really went down it?" The taller boy with dark brown hair asked in a reverent whisper.

The slighter boy, hair a bright copper red in the morning light, grinned and nodded. "I sure did. It was incredible."

Thomas licked his lips, suddenly parched, and glanced over his shoulder towards the far north field where his dad was working on a fence damaged by a tree in the last round of storms they'd had. "I dare you to do it again."

Joel's sky-blue eyes blazed as he shot back, "I dare *you*! I've already done it. It's your turn."

Thomas glanced over his shoulder again, feeling butterflies take flight in his stomach as he looked back down the steep slope of the hill. He eased his weight off the seat of his bike and felt gravity instantly try to pull the bike forward down the grade. He sat down, fighting the giddiness, and looked at Joel again, trying to project an utter lack of concern. "I said it first. In fact, I *double* dare you!"

"When's Trevor supposed to get here?" Brian asked.

Clancy, stuffing leaves and twigs around smaller limbs stacked for a fire, sat back on his heels and armed sweat off his forehead. "His dad was gonna drop him off after he got home from work. Guess he'll get here around seven or so."

"Why couldn't his mom bring him?" A head soon popped out of the nearby tent following the voice.

"Shoot," Clancy said, leaning back over his stack of wood and stuffing more leaves into the cracks. "His mom couldn't be bothered to run him out

1

here. I think it's stupid our parents wouldn't let us bring our own cars," he grumbled. It was a sore point for all of them but several of their parents weren't comfortable with the idea of their seventeen-year-old sons having access to unsupervised freedom for four whole days. Without a car there was little question of them leaving Big Clifty park, twelve miles from nowhere.

Michael continued out of the tent, pulling his stocky frame upright and flipping the tent flap closed. "Well, we should have a good dry spot to sleep tonight. Keep this flap shut and there won't be any bugs either." As he spoke, the zipper snagged on the nylon…like it always did…earning a barely audible "Shit!" as Michael backed the zipper off and then continued to ease it forward carefully.

"If he'd called me I could have had my mom stop by and pick him up," Brian, the loafer, scuffing his sneakers through some dead fall on the edge of the campsite, muttered.

Thomas came into the site with another armful of wood and dropped it off to the side, where they could get to it easily, yet safely away from the main fire pit. "I don't know about you guys, but I'm about ready to jump in that water."

All four heads swiveled to look at the blue water lapping gently along the rocky shoreline next to their campsite. An old frayed rope caught the breeze and swayed invitingly from the twisted oak perched among the boulders high above the water.

"Oh, hell yeah." Clancy was the first to respond, pulling his t-shirt off as he rose. The t-shirt was shortly followed by his denim shorts and then he raced for the rope. Soon, four teenage forms were flying through the air and splashing in various styles into the water. Clancy, the first to go, shot out as far as he could and landed feet first. Thomas, second, turned his into a graceful swan dive. Michael, the heaviest of the four, did a bomb, swamping Clancy and Thomas. Brian didn't bother with form and followed Clancy's example.

The water felt wonderful. It had been a hot day…one of the hottest so far this summer. The kind of mid-August day that makes you long for the cooler days of September and October just around the corner. Thomas had noticed that morning as he was dressing that the dogwood just outside his bedroom window was starting to sport a thin line of burgundy in the heart of the leaves. The first tease of fall to come. He leaned back and let himself float. The sun was hot on his closed eyelids and his chest, while his arms and legs floated in coolness.

"Hey, Thomas," Brian called out. "Some guy was in Hart's and I heard him ask Lyla if she knew you."

"Oh, yeah? What'd she say?"

"She told him yeah, she knew you."

The silence grew long and Thomas impatient. "Well…? And so…?"

"Just thought you'd want to know, is all. He asked if she knew where he might find you and she said she reckoned not. That's all."

"What'd he look like?"

"Hmmm. He was older. Like, maybe, in his late twenties? Kind of scruffy looking, I guess. Hadn't shaved in a while. Oh, and he had a tear drop tattoo under his eye. I noticed that."

"Hey!" Clancy jumped in. "Isn't that like a symbol you did time or something?"

"How would I know?" Thomas asked sharply.

Clancy shot him a frown. "Man, what's your deal? I thought I heard somewhere…"

"Well, maybe you did. So what? Anyway, doesn't sound like anyone I know. Hey…who wants to race me to that rock over there?"

"You're on, dude!" And Brian kicked off, getting an early lead, before Thomas even knew the race had started.

Dusk was settling through the trees and reflecting in the perfectly still water of the lake later that evening as the four boys made their first dinner. It would be the best meal they ate over the next four days since most of their moms had contributed. Thomas' mom sent premade hamburger patties loaded with onions and stuffed with cheddar cheese in the middle. Ten patties total for the five boys…they were expecting Trevor to show up at any time now. It was obvious Thomas' mom had talked to Clancy's mom who sent along the burger buns, lettuce leaves already washed and trimmed, sliced tomatoes in a plastic dish, and his cooler had mayonnaise, ketchup, mustard and pickles. Brian's mom threw in potato salad and a couple rolls of paper towels. Michael's mom hit the home run with the package of brownies loaded with pecans. They had supplies for the next three nights…packages of hot dogs, a package of sausage, potted meat spreads and tuna packets for lunches along with loaves of bread. Cans of beans and corn were stacked neatly in the locker box next to the tent along with matches and a bottle of fire starter. Two cases of water were stacked beside the locker along with two cases of soda. Bags of potato chips and other snacks shared space with the cans of vegetables, and it was a safe bet a lot of those cans would get trucked home unopened.

Thomas had just laid the first five burgers on the grill when they heard a motor slowly coming through the trees. They could just glimpse a flash of the dying light on glass or metal through the dense trees separating the campsite from the parking area. Within minutes another boy appeared through the trees, dragging a heavy duffel bag behind him, kicking dust up all around the edge of the camp area.

Thomas started flapping the metal spatula over the burgers to keep the dust away. "Trevor! Pick that bag up! We're all going to be eating dirt

3

burgers!"

"Oh, shoot! I didn't think…" Trevor, a tall lanky boy with a mop of dusty blonde hair who had a habit of flipping it back with a shake of his head…flipped his hair back now with a shake of his head.

"Trevor, my man! Glad you could make it!" Brian bounced up and slapped Trevor on his left shoulder. "Let me give you a hand with that. Were you able to score?"

"Was I able to score?" Trevor asked back, voice loaded with sarcasm. "Do the dogwoods bloom in spring? Of course, I scored! Twelve cold ones somewhere in the bottom of this freakin' heavy bag. Give me a hand with it, why don't you? Those burgers are smelling good, Thomas…don't let 'em burn. I'm starved!"

Thomas waved the spatula at him. "Go on. Get your bag put up…crack open those cold ones unless that's just another tall tale."

"That hurts, Thomas. Really hurts. You think I'd lie to you?" Trevor threw him a mock sad face and then burst into an irrepressible grin as Brian grabbed the other end of the duffel and pulled him towards the tent.

"Where'd you get the beer?" Clancy called after them.

"My old man. He figures I'm old enough to enjoy a cold one every once in a while. So long as my mom don't find out."

"Your dad's so cool, Trevor."

"Yeah, I guess so. Those burgers about ready, Thomas?"

"Almost. Get those buns over here, Michael, so I can throw them on for a minute."

Trevor, pulling a six-pack out of the duffel and tossing one to Clancy by the fire, hooted and said, "Careful, Michael! Thomas wants to toast your buns! Might not be a bad idea…plenty to go around!" He tossed a beer to Brian and then cracked one for himself.

"Hey, Trevor…don't be stingy. Where's a brew for Michael and me?" Thomas asked, checking the bun to be sure it wasn't burning.

"Just messin' with ya. Right here. Here, Michael…take this over to Thomas and grab one for yourself." Trevor held out the three remaining beers hanging from the plastic holder.

Soon, the five were sitting in a circle arranged around the fire, hunkering over their burgers and the chips they preferred to the potato salad. Brian picked up his can of beer and held it out to the others. "A toast," he announced. "Our fifth end of summer camping trip…been doing this for five years now…and I for one hope we do this every year for the rest of our lives. In fact, we should make a pact."

Clancy nodded eagerly and grabbed his can, as did the rest. "Oh, hell yes," he said. "Right here. We meet here for a four-night camping trip…just us guys. Which means, Trevor, you can't bring your current fling."

Everyone laughed, and cans clinked as the boys toasted. "Speaking of,"

Thomas began as they all sat back down, "how'd you manage to give Tanya the slip, Trevor? She's sort of been hanging pretty close to you this summer."

"Yeah. Honestly, it's been getting a bit old. I mean, it's always about her and what she wants to do. I don't think we'll be hanging out much longer. I get the third degree if I don't answer her texts right away. And…well, I just don't need that crap. We're gonna be seniors. Who wants to spend their last year in school tied down?" He flipped his hair back and shook his head, looking around the circle with a serious intensity. "There's time for that later, right?"

Brian shook his head. "I don't get it, Trevor. Tanya is smokin' hot, dude. Have you thought this through?"

Trevor laughed sarcastically, tossing his hair back, "I've thought of little else here lately. Another good reason it's time to break it off. Burgers were good, Thomas. Hit the spot!" He leaned back and tilted his beer, draining the last of it.

Thomas nodded at Clancy. "What about you, Clance? You still seeing Sandy?"

"Clancy and Sandy, sitting by a tree, f – u – c – k – I – n - g! First she gets pregnant and then they get married!" Brian sang out in sing song.

"Shut up!" Clancy snarled, then gave a half shrug and nod to Thomas. "Yeah, I'm still seeing her. She's pretty cool to hang with sometimes."

Thomas nodded…as if he knew…wishing he did. He was too terrified to talk to girls. The ones he knew anyway, were pretty intimidating. He had no idea what to talk to them about.

Brian, a little bruised with the tone Clancy had taken with him, turned on Michael, easy prey. "Are you still mooning around over Autumn, Michael?"

Dusk had settled into night around the campsite as they ate dinner but the flush that stole over Michael's face was obvious even in the shadows and fire play. "No." His tone was sullen, knowing he was the brunt of something else once again and not happy. "Hey, Trevor," he called, "you brought a second six-pack, didn't you?"

"Yeah," Trevor replied. "I threw it in that blue cooler over there. Why don't you grab us each another one? Not enough to go for threefers. You'll all have to settle for a twofer tonight. Not to worry, though. My old man might sneak me some out tomorrow afternoon."

"That would be awesome, man!" Thomas weighed in.

"What about you, Thomas? You got a shine on anyone? I heard Melissa Paulson's sweet on you. She's real cute. Got a nice wrack on her, too, if you don't mind my sayin' so."

"And if I did? Mind?" Thomas responded.

Trevor shrugged. "Guess that'd be your problem then…not mine!" And he laughed, popping the top on the new beer Michael handed him. "By the way, ran into someone who said they was looking for you."

"Oh?" Thomas popped the top on his can, taking a long swig from the beer. "Someone was in Hart's looking for me, too."

"This guy wanted to know where you lived. I told him I couldn't say, but if he had a message, I'd be glad to pass it along. He said he did."

"Yeah? So, what's the message?" Thomas was irritated, not appreciating the head games Trevor liked to play, stringing things out to get maximum drama.

"He said to tell you he'd be at Chaser's next Saturday night and you should meet him there. At around eight."

"Hmmm." Thomas took another drink, a cold weight settling into his stomach not entirely due to the beer.

"Oh," Trevor added, "He said one more thing. Alone. Come alone." Trevor leaned back in his folding chair and drank from his beer, then gazed at Thomas across the fire. "So, what gives, man? What's this guy want with you?"

Thomas ran a hand through his hair, setting his empty paper plate on the ground beside him and leaning over towards the fire. "What did this guy look like?"

Trevor shrugged. "I don't know. He was older...maybe in his mid or late twenties, I guess. I'm no good at guessing ages. I just know he was older. He had dirty blonde hair, real shaggy. Lot of scruff. Hadn't shaved in a couple days, that's for sure. Stubble was a bit darker than his hair...more brown."

Brian, sitting to Thomas' right, started nodding vigorously. "Yeah. Yeah, man. That's the guy I saw in Hart's."

"What else?" Thomas asked.

Trevor flipped his hair back, drank some more of his beer and said, "He had a tattoo. A teardrop under his left eye. Just one...a single teardrop. I think that means you did time. Or you killed someone. Or both. Hell, I'm not sure." He drained the last of his can. "Hey, Michael! If you grab me one of those last two brews you can have the last one yourself!"

Clancy groaned. "Trevor, that's not fair! We could have played a hand for it...you know, winner gets the last beer."

Trevor laughed. "No! The way it would go is I'd finish this one and drink that one too!"

Michael grinned and grabbed his bounty.

"So, really, Thomas. Who is this guy? What does he want?" Clancy asked, growing serious.

Thomas frowned and ran his hand through his hair again, thick brown waves bouncing back as he passed his hand through. "I think...he sounds about the right age. I can't be sure though." He sighed and sat back. "It's a long story."

Brian shrugged, "Gonna be a long night. What else we doing?"

Clancy snickered and Michael giggled. "Tell us, Thomas. And if you need help next Saturday, I don't give a shit what that guy said…you don't have to walk in there alone." Trevor braved.

"When I was seven this kid Joel moved in next door." Thomas started.

"Oh, hey!" Michael burst out. "Joel Allen! I remember him. Didn't he die the summer of fifth grade or something?"

Thomas nodded. "Yeah, he died. We were nine…and it was the fall of fourth grade."

Michael mused, "Weren't you guys close? I seem to remember you hanging out all the time in grade school."

"From that first summer, yeah. It was July when they bought that place two houses down from my house. Sat back from the road just around the curve going towards 23."

It was hot, and Thomas was bored. He'd already hit the three baseballs he had and retrieved them each about four times now. The sun beating down and the dust motes floating from the field next door where his father was baling hay soon took any fun out of swinging at the balls. He dropped them in the canvas backpack he toted and looked around the yard for something to do. His dusty black bike leaned invitingly against the garage door wall. His dad had said he could ride down the drive and as far up the road as where the guardrail started as long as he only went left out of the drive and never to the right. There was a steep hill to the right and his mom was terrified he'd wreck on it.

He dropped the backpack next to the door and wheeled the bike around the dusty dirt in front of the entrance to their detached garage. His mom had gone to town to get groceries and his sister, Lisa, had gone with her. He wished now he'd gone along, too. Mom would probably stop at that little coffee shop on the way out of town and let Lisa get something. He thought about a frosty, cold drink with lots of whipped cream, and decided that next time he'd go along, too.

Their drive was relatively short, and he soon reached the hard paving of the road and hooked a left on the shoulder. The guardrail started on a curve about a quarter of a mile further down the road, heading uphill. Thomas stood on the pedals to get up some speed, leaning out over his handle bars. A woodpecker was busy hammering in the woods across the road and his father's tractor droned amidst the dust cloud obscuring it from view. Thomas could feel a little breeze on his forehead now and leaned closer to the handlebars, offering less resistance, his legs scissoring like mad to get up the hill. The ride up was hard but the payoff was in the ride back. He could pick up speed…maybe get up to as much as ten miles an hour by the time he reached their drive coming back down. After that he'd head inside and find a snack. Maybe some peanut butter and crackers.

Thomas had just reached the guardrail and brought his bike to a stop, wheeling it around to prepare for the ride home, when he heard someone shout, "Hey! Hey, you! Hi! Hold up!"

Thomas looked around and saw another boy on a bike at the far end of the curve, coming towards him. He straddled his bike and watched over his shoulder as the other boy approached. Soon he pulled up beside him. "Hey! Hi! I'm Joel Allen. Just moved in next door." He jerked his chin over his right shoulder back the way he'd just come.

"Oh, yeah," Thomas replied. "You musta moved into the old Lloyd place. It that brown and white house just down that way?" He pointed back up the hill along the guardrail.

Joel nodded. "Yeah. I don't know the name of who owned it before but me and my folks moved in about two weeks ago. What's your name?"

"Oh. Thomas."

"You live around here?" Joel asked.

Thomas guessed they were about the same age. Joel had a shock of bright carrot red hair and the complexion that went with it. He was a painful looking red in the hot sun. "Yeah. I live right down there." He waved toward his driveway. "That's a bad burn you got."

Joel grinned. "Yeah. My dad took us out on the boat last weekend and I got fried."

Thomas perked up. "You got a boat?"

"Sure do," Joel said. "It's fast, too. Real fast." He nodded wisely, as though he had great experience at judging the speed of boats.

"I'm seven," Thomas offered. "How old are you?"

"Cool!" Joel hooped. "I'm seven too! We'll be in the same grade in school, I bet. I'll be starting second next month."

Thomas nodded, "Yeah, me too."

Suddenly they heard a motor coming and within minutes a car appeared on the hill above, heading towards them. Thomas quickly walked his bike to the edge so Joel would be behind him, recognizing his mom's silver Mustang. He waved at her as she went by and his sister Lisa stuck her tongue out, holding up a drink carton and showing him the whipped cream on the top of her tongue.

Thomas turned back to Joel. "Well, hey…it's nice to meet you. That was my mom. I gotta go help get in groceries. I guess I'll see you around."

"You got a phone?" Joel asked.

"Yeah. My dad don't let me talk on it much, though. I mean, you can call. Numbers 253-9359."

"OK. Think your folks would let you come over?"

Thomas shrugged. "I don't know. I'll ask."

"Cool. That'd be sweet. My dad's putting up a basketball hoop if you want to play some."

"OK. Sounds fun." Thomas lined his bike up again along the white line staying inside the shoulder. "Well, gotta run. Talk to you later!" He was heading down the hill by the time the last word escaped and starting to pick up speed. He pedaled even faster, feeling the air rushing past, feeling almost like he could fly. He reached his drive and smoothly swerved into it, carefully riding the high side of the gully rain had worn into the right-hand side. His mom was continually complaining about that gully and his dad kept telling her he'd get to it. She already had the first round of bags trucked into the house by the time he propped his bike next to the garage wall.

"I could use a hand here, Thomas." His mom called. "And what did I tell you about picking up after yourself?" She arched an eyebrow at the abandoned backpack.

"I know. I'll get it."

"Who was that boy you were talking to?" She reached into the trunk of the car, pulling out two more bags while Lisa came strolling up behind her.

"Said his name's Joel Allen. His folks bought the Lloyd place. He asked if I could come over to play some basketball."

"Oh! Well, that'll be nice!"

"Oh, yes, won't it?" Lisa crooned, rolling her eyes. "Just what was missing around here was another annoying seven-year-old. He doesn't have a sister my age, does he?"

Thomas shrugged. "Don't know." She loved every opportunity of rubbing in the fact that she was four years' older…almost a fabled teenager herself at eleven.

Thomas took the last swig out of his can, scowling at the bitter taste of the now lukewarm and flat beer. It had been a long time since he'd talked about Joel. He was relieved that it was easier than he'd thought it would be. Maybe the therapy he'd started attending when he was eleven had helped. "We became best buds that summer he moved in next door. He was real wild, though…always wanting to break the rules. Got a kick if he could do something that he knew he wasn't supposed to."

Clancy nodded. "I remember that. He was that way in school, too. If the teacher turned her back he'd be the one pulling a prank."

Thomas smiled, "Yeah. He was good at that. D'you recall the time he put the wad of duct tape on Ms. Wells' chair and when she stood up it ripped her skirt? Golly was she embarrassed with her skirt hanging half down her butt."

Trevor was laughing hard, holding his side and nodding vigorously. "I'd forgotten about that! Oh, that was so friggin' awesome."

Slowly the group grew more somber, remembering the story didn't end well.

"You all know that steep hill past my house when you head to War Eagle? Well, my folks wouldn't let me ride my bike down that hill. It's really dangerous. First of all, the grade is pretty steep and it's at least three eighths of a mile before it starts to flatten out. The entire descent curves just slightly to the left. Then, when you get to the bottom and it starts to flatten…well, it hooks a hard righthand turn…a hairpin…around a rock bluff. The shoulder between the road and the bluff isn't more than two feet wide. It's completely blind. You can't see if anything is coming at you. You can't hear it either. On the other side the hill is pretty steep, and it's piled up with big rocks. At the bottom of that is a tangled weedy mess with a little shit creek that's more mud than water." Thomas' eyes had grown into a fixed stare, glaring at the heart of the fire, not seeing the leaping flames but reliving a long-ago day.

Michael cleared his throat and scuffed his foot, the silence dragging out uncomfortably, feeling like he needed to do something to break the tension. He released a belch; a deep basal belch brought on more from nervousness than from beer consumption.

Thomas jerked and laughed, "Awesome, dude. That was completely awesome."

The rest of the group laughed, and Trevor said, "Hold that thought, man…I've got to relieve a little pressure."

"I did it!" Joel declared triumphantly.

"Oh, yeah? What's that?" Thomas asked, squinting hard at the bug he was pinning to the poster board for the science class project they were working on.

"You gotta guess."

Thomas glanced up, the bug securely pinned to the board. "Okay. Let's see…you got a B in math?" They'd just gotten their first progress reports, and Thomas knew Joel had been nervous about taking his home. His dad expected nothing less than B's and Joel was pretty certain he'd gotten a C in math.

"Nah. Nothing like that." He smirked, and Thomas silently chided himself for thinking Joel might be this excited about a good grade.

"You got to the next level on *Call of Duty*?"

"I wish. Man, this level is hard. I keep getting killed right after you come out of that tunnel…"

Thomas was stumped and down to his last guess. "I don't know…"

"I rode *the hill*…"

He said it with something like reverence and his sky-blue eyes blazed. "You gotta do it. It was…" He shrugged expressively and shook his head. "It was awesome! That turn makes you go fast! And when you get to the bottom, you've got to lay it over to catch that right. I held it in the lane…no one was coming…but even if there had been I'da been all right. That bluff felt like it was right there off my shoulder…what a rush!"

Thomas stared at his friend, conflicted with excitement and fear. "Cool," he breathed in response.

"C'mon, man. You gotta do this with me…. just once. I dare you."

Thomas shook his head, opening a bottle of water, as Trevor settled back into his spot. He looked around at his circle of friends, friends he'd grown up with and shared all his secrets with. It occurred to him that he'd never really opened up to them the way they'd been open with him. They did not know this story even after all these years. And feeling the twinge of guilt, ever present, he knew they would never know the whole story. He could only share so much…even now.

Brian popped the top on a soda and said, "I know the turn you're talking about. That's where Trevor got in trouble with his dad for throwing rocks at that old barn that sits on the outside of that turn."

Thomas nodded quickly. "Yes. Just before you come to the turn there's a dirt lane that leads off and an old barn on the corner. It's mostly falling to pieces."

Brian grinned. "Yeah. You could say Trevor was giving it a hand. Only his dad caught him at it."

"It wasn't fair," Trevor grumbled. "You and Thomas were both there and as I remember it you both threw your share of rocks…"

Brian laughed. "*We* didn't get caught!"

Thomas smiled along with them and resumed his story, "Yeah. That's the turn. I didn't agree right away. I think it was around September when that happened. I know we hadn't been back in school too long and we were collecting things like grasshoppers, so it couldn't have been much later than that."

He drank deeply from the water bottle and gazed again deep into the flame. Going back to the late warm October day when he was nine years old. The memory was crystalline, every detail still engraved…

The sun was coming up behind Joel and his hair gleamed a dark auburn with glints of bright copper as a ray of morning sunlight struck the back of his head. *Hunh. It's gotten a lot darker,* Thomas thought, recalling how it had been carrot red two years ago when they'd met. He stood astride his bike at the head of the hill. The early October day was unseasonably warm, close to eighty already at ten o'clock in the morning; the air heavy with humidity and perfectly still…not a breath of a breeze. Thunderstorms were forecast for later that evening and you could feel the tension in the air. Beads of sweat glistened in the small fine hairs on Joel's cheek. He grinned at Thomas. "Now, remember. I'll go first. You wait until I come back around the turn and you can see me at the bottom. I'll signal you when it's safe to go."

Someone standing at the bottom, at the head of a small dirt lane that turned off to the left beside an old barn, would have a view of the other side of the turn for at least a small distance. Not all the way around, no real certainty that a car might not appear in the next second.

Thomas wished he could say he had begged him not to go. Instead he had thrown up his right hand, "Put it there and I'll see you at the bottom." They high-fived and Thomas kicked his bike over on its kickstand and went to stand behind Joel, straddling the back wheel. Joel wanted a sendoff, so he could get up even more speed. Thomas grabbed the back of the seat and then counted it out.

"One!" He pulled back on the seat and then rocked Joel forward a nudge.

"Two!" Rock and nudge.

"Three!" And he pulled *hard* and gave an even harder shove forward, really leaning into it. Joel took off like a rocket...too fast, the front wheel wobbling as the back over-powered it...Thomas' heart leaping into his throat as he expected to watch Joel spill across the pavement. Instead, Joel leveled out, crouching low behind the handlebars, hugging into the frame, knees pumping. Thomas would never forget that sight. He flew. Joel really flew that day. He had to be doing thirty-five when he hit the bottom. He laid it over on the right, but he was a second too late doing it and the bike drifted out. Just as Thomas lost sight of him, he knew Joel had crossed left of center.

Time does funny things at moments like this. It seemed like suddenly it stopped. Thomas heard a long squeal as rubber tried, and failed, to stop on hot pavement. He heard a crunch, barely audible. It happened so fast, the sound almost insignificant compared to the sound of those tires. Then stillness. Complete and utter silence; even the insects pausing for a moment in their endless susurration.

Thomas drew in a trembling breath and held it for a moment. "Then I broke into a run," he resumed. "Tearing down that hill as fast as I could. It never occurred to me to ride my bike. I don't know how long it took me to reach the bottom...maybe thirty seconds?" He shook his head. "I heard a motor and here comes an old slightly rusted car...a Nova...around the turn. It's got a hell of a dent in the hood. Windshield's busted. Drove right by...guy never even looked at me. I watched. I got his license plate."

"Oh, shit," Brian breathed quietly, and Thomas pulled his gaze away from the fire, looking around at his circle of friends.

"You were there!" Clancy said, something close to horror in his voice.

Thomas nodded. "Yeah. After the car passed, I ran around the curve...the bike was there...what was left of it. I guess the impact threw Joel over the rail...I found him in the weeds at the bottom of the berm." His eyes filled unexpectedly with tears. Angrily, he dashed them away. "He was still alive then. I wasn't sure what to do...I didn't want to leave him. I'd seen on TV that you aren't supposed to move injured folks, but they do it all the time on the news...pulling folks from burning cars...ya know? I didn't know what to do. Well, I heard a car coming and I ran up and flagged it down. It was a guy from town who'd been over shopping in Rogers. He called for an ambulance. I think they declared Joel dead at the hospital. My folks kept me home, because of the news crews…so I'm not sure how long he might have lived…after." His voice trailed off and he finished the bottle of water, tossing the empty into the bag they had hung from a tree on the far side of the camp site.

"It was a hit and run," Clancy said gravely, perhaps the only one fully comprehending what that meant.

"Yeah," Thomas nodded. Gazing back into the fire. "His name was Pete Barrett."

"And this guy…the one with the tear drop…he's the one that killed Joel? You think it's Pete Barrett?" It was no surprise that Michael had caught up quickly.

Thomas nodded in agreement again. It was fully dark now and the shadows pressed in close around the fire, the lake sparkling under a quarter waxing moon. "I gave the police the license plate and a description. I got a pretty good look at him when he drove by me. The police had him locked up by that night. He got ten years for involuntary manslaughter and for leaving the scene. He'd been smoking dope, I heard. As a juvie I wasn't allowed to attend court…they used a deposition instead of me appearing. He didn't fight it. He never denied it. Said he was going to turn himself in anyway." Thomas shrugged and got another water out of the cooler.

"Wow." Trevor said. "That's some pretty heavy shit. And you think this guy's looking for you now?"

Thomas shrugged again and said, a little drily, "I can't think of too many other convicts that might be looking for me."

That last week of summer vacation was the longest, and shortest, that Thomas could remember. The weekend at Beaver Lake had flown by quickly while each day had seemed to last forever. The boys spent endless hours in the blue water and flirted with the girls that brought paddle boards out Saturday and Sunday morning. Monday afternoon arrived quickly. Trevor's dad showed up around three, and all five piled in the cab of the truck after throwing their gear in the bed.

On Tuesday, Thomas returned to his job at New Delhi Café, where he worked the lunch shift Tuesday through Saturday. This would be his last week working there and probably his last time *ever* working there since he'd be graduating this year. It was the first time in his life that Thomas had ever really thought about things so finally. His *last* year of school, *last* summer working at New Delhi. His entire life up to this point had been about tomorrow's…an endless stream of them it had seemed, before school would end. Now that end was in sight and Thomas was surprised that he felt a tinge of sorrow at the thought. There was no question he was excited and ready to put school behind him…but for the first time he experienced a sense that he was also losing something. Losing his easy youthful days and the comfort of the routines of childhood. He blamed his melancholy on the memories of Joel he had dredged up, stirring up emotions he'd put a lid on year's ago.

Each passing day found the tension in Thomas building. What did the man want with him? Thomas could imagine how he must have hated him for turning him in. He'd been in jail for the past eight years, which meant he had gotten out early. It had been a ten-year sentence. What did that say about him? Was he a good guy? Or did he want revenge? It was all too easy to imagine him sitting in jail for almost three thousand days building up resentment and a need for retribution against the boy that had turned him in.

Thomas woke early on Saturday. It was a few minutes before six and the light outside his west facing bedroom window was barely enough to lighten the thick haze of dense fog pressing against the glass. Rising on his elbow he peered at his clock and groaned, collapsing back on his pillow in frustration. It was going to be a long day and he had hoped he'd sleep in. He stared at the ceiling for a few minutes and then swung his legs out of bed, figuring he might as well get up. Maybe he could run a couple miles and then get breakfast, work off some of this nervous energy he'd built up.

He rose and stood at his window, seeing his own ghostly reflection in the glass as the gray fog pressed against the other side, turning the shapes of trees into dark and ominous figures looming just beyond sight. It was eerily similar to that October morning long ago. That morning had also had a heavy fog, burned off quickly by the morning sun so that only wisps remained when the two boys met at the top of the hill at ten.

Thomas thought again of that morning, bitter with himself for withholding the full truth from his friends. The weight of his guilt pressed against the walls of his chest, filling him with despair. It was possible, if he hadn't called the double dare that Joel wouldn't have gone. It was possible it might have been Thomas that went…should have been Thomas. Joel *had* originally dared Thomas…that September afternoon when Thomas had sat pinning a dead bug to a piece of board. Thomas shook his head, trying to dislodge the thought. So many things were possible in life yet didn't happen. This was no different from a thousand other decisions he made daily.

His eyes met the gaze of his ghost-self eyes in the glass as he reflected that that may be true, but his daily decisions didn't carry the same dire consequences. When it had really counted, when a decision had never been more important before or since…he had failed. And he continued to fail. He had never been able to share the full truth, the real horror, even with the psychiatrists his parents had sent him to. Now, most recently, with the friends that knew him best, knew every secret of his teenage years, he was unable to admit the full weight of his guilt. Shaking his head again, Thomas looked down at the wooden floorboards between his feet, his shoulders sagging unconsciously with the burden of his desolation, running a hand through his tousled hair and turning to face the long day ahead.

That workday seemed endless. Every time the bell tinkled when the door opened, he found himself jerking and looking, expecting to see a man with a tear drop tattoo coming through the entrance. It was illogical, of course. It was unlikely Pete would recognize Thomas even if he did come in. Thomas recalled too clearly the way Pete had stared fixedly straight ahead as he had crept past him, slowly gaining momentum up the steep hill. He had not looked at the young boy panting heavily from his run down the slope, narrow chest heaving under the thin cotton t-shirt. That young boy bore little resemblance to the toned young man he had developed into. They had only seen each other the one time.

At two o'clock Thomas turned in his final timesheet and shook the owner's hand. "I'm really going to miss you. I've enjoyed working here."

His boss smiled warmly, pumping his hand vigorously. "I've enjoyed having you here. Anytime you need a recommendation, you can use me. You've got a good work ethic. You'll go far, you build on that." He reviewed Thomas' timesheet and wrote a check, signing with a flourish. Thomas grinned when he saw the season-end bonus that had been added.

The heat hit him as he stepped out onto the hot pavement, glancing at his watch. Only quarter after two. He still had almost five hours before he had to be at Chaser's. Feeling restless, his stomach full of acid and churning, muscles jittery and tense, he didn't want to drive home and try to sit or search for something to do to pass the time. He needed a distraction. Remembering that Michael would be working in the kitchen at Chelsea's he turned and headed up the stairs to Center Street. He'd drop by and visit with Michael, maybe lend a hand with the dishes. The manager didn't care...he got free labor.

Michael was a good foil for the dark thoughts that hovered on the edges of Thomas' awareness. He kept Thomas laughing with funny stories about his two younger sisters, aged thirteen and eleven. The thirteen-year-old, Lou, saw herself as too old to suffer the company of the younger girl, Nikki. Nikki thought otherwise and followed Lou everywhere. The two fought constantly and some of their exchanges were pretty epic to hear Michael tell it. He was old enough that they didn't drag him into their conflicts and they both looked at him with something close to awe...he was almost through school! He was amused by their competitiveness.

The afternoon passed pleasantly, and it was soon five-thirty. The boys walked slowly back down to where Thomas had left his truck. They still had another hour to kill before they were to meet Clancy and Trevor at Chaser's. They had all agreed to meet there at seven.

"You got your poles in back?" Michael asked as Thomas unlocked the doors of his small Ford Ranger. It was used and had been pretty beat up when Thomas bought it, but it was his pride and joy. He kept the oil changed and his dad helped him with his seasonal maintenance.

"Yep. Wanna go out to the lake and toss a few?"

"Sure." Michael slid heavily into the passenger seat and Thomas headed back through town, turning onto Benton to cut over to Oil Spring Road.

As he eased the truck down the old dirt road, Michael asked, "Are you nervous about tonight?"

Thomas shrugged and shifted the truck to a lower gear. It had rained heavily the day before and there were some slick spots. "Yeah. I guess so."

Michael nodded. "Yeah. Me too."

Thomas threw him a glance and replied, "You know, I appreciate you guys wanting to be there and all but you know you don't have to."

Michael shot him back a surprised look, "No way I'm not going!"

Thomas grinned, "Okay. Just so long as you know I'd be cool if you didn't."

The next hour passed pleasantly while the boys threw lures into the still waters of the small lake. Neither got a bite and it was hot under the late summer sun. Insects droned, and Thomas was able for a short while to forget about the coming evening until Michael said quietly, "Well, I guess we'd better head that way."

The molten ball of lead in Thomas' stomach turned over and he felt jittery again. Glancing at his watch and seeing that it was quarter to seven he nodded. "Yeah. Come on."

Clancy and Trevor weren't at Chaser's yet when Thomas and Michael pulled into the parking lot. The place looked mostly deserted and Thomas' heart sank. He'd been hoping the place would be busy, a lot of cars in the parking lot. All he saw now were two Harley's leaning on their pegs next to the main door and a brown Toyota pickup parked at the far back. Probably the bartender's or someone who worked there. Trevor pulled up in his white Mustang five minutes later, grinning and throwing a wave as he pulled into the spot next to Thomas.

"Well, are we ready?" Trevor asked cheerfully as the four walked to the door.

"You bet!" Michael responded gamely.

"Now, remember, Trevor," Thomas said urgently as they entered the cool dark interior of the club, "He might recognize you. It would be best if we didn't sit together. I need to sit by myself."

"Sure!" Trevor said. "I was thinking we'd sit over by the pool table and play pool. I got a roll of quarters when I took my paycheck to the bank earlier. I thought you could sit at the next table or something. Act like we just met...I don't know..."

Thomas nodded. "Yeah. That'd work."

"You hungry?" Clancy asked.

"Not really." Thomas responded. "I might eat some fries."

"I'm hungry," Michael threw in.

"You're always hungry!" Trevor said, giving Michael's substantial belly a playful slap.

"Stop it!" Michael cried, jerking away angrily.

"Give it up," Thomas muttered, more anger than he'd intended in his voice.

Trevor threw his hands up, palms out, "Okay. Cool. Just havin' a little fun, is all."

Slowly the little bar began filling up. Thomas sat at the table in the far corner near the restrooms while Clancy, Trevor and Michael chose the table next to his. Michael ordered a burger and onion rings, Clancy settled for a plate of loaded fries and Trevor got a pulled pork sandwich with coleslaw. The sight and smell of the food when it arrived sickened Thomas and he felt his stomach roll. He nursed a large Coke rather than eat. Each time the door opened, he'd tense and look at Trevor. After checking out the new arrival, Trevor would shake his head. Not yet.

Thomas watched a group of three biker types come in and belly up to the bar. Shortly after that a young couple hanging all over each other came in and headed for the outdoor patio seating area. At seven thirty the band members started arriving and hauling in their equipment, setting things up on the small stage area between the pool tables and outdoor seating.

While the band members were coming and going, a guy with a crew cut and wraparound sunglasses came in and Thomas looked at Trevor. Trevor was lining up to shoot his striped ball in the corner pocket. After taking, and missing, the shoot, he stood back and studied the newcomer. Thomas waited tensely until he saw the small negative shake of the head as Trevor strolled back to his table to get a sip of his soda while Clancy decided on his next shot.

Thomas finished his Coke and looked around the shadowy interior. It was filling up. He caught the waitress's eye and raised his glass to her. She nodded, came across to grab his glass and got him a refill. Thomas turned the sweating glass on the cardboard coaster, watching water droplets collect until gravity pulled them down, soaking a circle into the already damp square of pressed paper. What did the guy want with him? Surely, he didn't plan anything violent with so many people around. He caught Michael watching him from the next table and Thomas frowned at him. Quickly Michael averted his eyes, fixing them on the pool table instead.

Thomas felt a surge of nerves as the door opened and a man with shoulder length hair and a wild looking beard filled the door frame. Anxiously, Thomas looked at Trevor only to find he was over at the jukebox feeding quarters in, his back to the door. Thomas looked again at the man who had just entered but as he crossed into the glow of the hanging lights over the pool tables it was obvious this man wasn't sporting any tattoos on his face. Thomas slumped, wrapping his hands around the cold glass and taking a sip of the sugary soda. Suddenly he felt an urgent need to urinate. Grimly he pushed his chair back and headed for the restroom.

As the door closed behind him it shut out the increasing noise from the bar. The bathroom was small and suddenly hushed. Thomas couldn't at first seem to release the pressure in his bladder and stood there looking at the wall over the urinal in discomfort. Finally, a tiny trickle dribbled out, and Thomas understood that it was only his nerves making him feel like he had to go. He crossed to the sink and plunged his hands under the cold water, scooping some up to splash over his face. Reaching for the towel dispenser mounted on the wall next to the sink, he heard the bathroom door open behind him. Quickly drying his face on the towel he looked in the mirror over the sink and saw the man with the crew cut and sunglasses standing over his shoulder.

"Excuse me," he mumbled, reaching for another towel to finish drying his hands. As he did so he saw the man reflected in the mirror reach to remove his sunglasses. As the man's left hand came down, grasping the edges of the frames, Thomas clearly saw the tear drop tattooed under the man's left eye. He felt a stab of pain in his stomach and his bladder again felt over full. He leaned forward into the sink and his eyes locked with the cool gaze of the stranger as he casually leaned back against the closed door.

"You Thomas?" It came out almost like a growl, the man's voice low and rumbling in his muscular chest.

Thomas turned to face him, leaning the small of his back against the sink basin. "Yeah.' He was surprised to hear his voice come out clear and seemingly calm.

"Thought I asked you to come alone?" The man had brown eyes and those eyes were drilling into Thomas' with intensity.

Thomas felt a flush start to creep up his cheeks, his skin growing warm. "I am alone," he replied defensively. "Who are you? What do you want?"

The man looked Thomas over and shifted his weight, crossing his arms over his chest. "Name's Pete." He reached into his breast pocket and Thomas tensed, but he only pulled out a can of snuff and casually opened the lid, pinching off a small bit which he packed into his lower lip. His brown eyes returned to meet Thomas'. "I just want to talk to you."

"Well, this ain't exactly the place to have a conversation," Thomas said a little lamely, gesturing around the small bathroom, corners dim in the weak glow of bare yellow bulb hanging from the ceiling.

Pete shrugged, "Reckon not. You're friends out there going to cause me any trouble?"

Thomas shook his head. "Not unless they need to." He hoped so, anyway.

Pete nodded. "In that case, why don't I come join you at your table and you and me can have a little chat. That sound okay with you?"

Thomas swallowed, feeling like he had a bone lodged in his throat, "Sure."

Pete stepped away from the door and gave Thomas room to step past him. "I'll be out in just a minute," he promised.

Thomas exited the bathroom, stepping into the sudden wash of sound from the bar. The tones of a woman's laughter floated over the deeper rumble of many male voices speaking in a cacophony of sound. He heard the sharp click as pool balls collided and the whine of feedback as someone on the stage toyed with the bass guitar. *Free Bird* belted out of the jukebox laying down a soundtrack almost drowning out the rest of the noise.

Thomas headed for his table and leaned over the back of Clancy's chair, whispering urgently into his friends' ear. "He's here. I just ran into him in the bathroom. He knows about you guys, too."

Clancy jerked as if Thomas had hit him and looked at him in surprise. "What?"

Thomas nodded and sat down in his seat quickly, taking a long sip from his soda, his throat suddenly dry and scratchy. He caught the glow of the bathroom light as the door opened and turned his attention back to Pete as he exited the gloom of the short hallway. Pete crossed back over to the bar where he picked up a glass of beer and came over to Thomas' table. He indicated the chair across from Thomas, "This okay?"

Thomas nodded and pulled his glass closer, hunching over the laminated round table. Pete sat down and the two gazed at each other until Thomas began to feel uncomfortable under the steady stare of the other man. "So, what did you want to talk about?" Thomas tried to sound casual but the slight tremble on the final word betrayed his tension. He cleared his throat.

Pete contemplated his glass of beer and then took a long drink from it. He lowered the glass to the table. "Stuff used to taste better." He nodded towards the glass and then met Thomas' eyes again. "I guess you develop a taste for it."

Thomas frowned, not sure what to say, confused.

Pete sighed and leaned back in his chair, running a hand over his close-cropped hair. "Feels funny," he gave a short chuckle to support his statement. "I just got my hair cut off today. Once they trimmed it when I went to jail, before going to court, I decided I wouldn't cut it again until I got out."

Again, the steady stare across the short distance separating them. Again, Thomas could not sustain Pete's steady glare and lowered his eyes to his glass of soda, peeking quickly towards his friends to see if they were watching. Trevor was standing on the other side of the pool table, gripping his pool cue tightly and watching Pete intently. Clancy was leaning over to shoot but his eyes were on Pete, not the balls on the table. Michael was picking at the plate of food still in front of him, studying Pete as he absently munched on the remaining pieces of fried onion rings. None of them were being exactly subtle about their interest. Grimly Thomas looked back at Pete and was surprised to find him smiling. He frowned quizzically.

Pete shifted in his chair and leaned forward on his forearms. "Dude, relax." He actually chuckled as he took another drink from his beer, "I really just want to talk. Truth is," he hesitated, his eyes catching and holding Thomas' gaze, "I want to say I'm sorry."

"Hunh?" The casually thrown apology took Thomas completely by surprise.

Pete looked down and nodded. "I have relived that day every day for the past eight years."

He looked up and Thomas searched his face in disbelief.

"What? Did you think I had it in for you?"

He could hear incredulity in Pete's tone. He felt his cheeks flush again as he nodded, not able to speak with the lump of fear still lodged in his throat.

This time Pete did laugh, leaning back and bracing his hands on his thighs. Thomas saw Clancy pull up in surprise and all three of his friends looked over inquiringly at Thomas. Thomas gave a tiny head shake and little shrug, indicating his confusion.

Pete's laugh trickled off to a chuckle which tapered off into silence as they once again gazed at each other. The tiny tear drop had been done crudely and up-close Thomas could see the edges weren't done cleanly, the tear drop wobbled a little to one side. As if feeling the weight of Thomas' eyes, Pete brushed his fingers lightly over the tattoo. "My souvenir for time served." He folded his large hands around his beer glass and looked somberly down at them. "A reminder of what I did. If I could go back…"

Thomas heard Pete's voice choke up. He sipped from his soda and kept quiet. Let Pete do the talking.

Pete shook his head. "I'd gotten stoned that morning. I had a job working out at Lake Leatherwood and decided I'd get high before I went in. I don't know if that made a difference…I don't think so. There was no time, even if I had been completely sober. I mean, I don't think there's anything I could or would have done that might have made it end differently. I was coming into that turn and all at once he was there. In my lane. It happened so fast."

Thomas could hear the earnestness in Pete's voice. He could hear pain, as well.

"I should have stopped." Now Pete's eyes drilling into Thomas' revealed the full depth of his despair. "I was afraid. I didn't know what to do and I panicked."

Thomas couldn't help himself, "You left him there to die." He could hear the angry condemnation in his whispered words.

This time it was Pete that dropped his eyes and looked away. He nodded miserably. "Yes," his voice almost a whisper. "Yes, I left him there to die. And part of me died with him." His eyes lifted again, meeting Thomas with a desperate hunger. "I need you to know that. I need you to understand that."

Thomas didn't understand. He could only return Pete's look as he struggled to sort out the emotions surging through him. He felt the release of tension as his fear drained away while a sudden surge of anger took root in its place. This time when he shook his head, he did so forcefully. "It was wrong." He asserted. "What you did was just wrong."

Pete nodded, "I know that. That's what I'm trying to tell you. I was wrong, I know I was wrong and I'm so sorry. If I could go back…if I could have a do-over, don't you think I would?" His tone was pleading, begging Thomas for empathy.

And despite himself, Thomas realized that he did understand. He leaned back weakly, suddenly realizing all of his strength had drained out along with all of his anger. He felt empty and his burden of guilt was greater than ever. He studied Pete across the table from him.

Pete toyed with a soggy napkin soaking up the pooling drops of water condensing off his glass. He drained the last of the beer and pushed the glass away. "Well, that's what I came to say to you. I won't be hanging around these parts. Figure I'll head towards Colorado, west coast maybe. Blows my mind that weed is legal in some states since I've been in the pen." He shook his head wonderingly and rose to his feet. He dropped a ten dollar bill on the table, placing his empty glass on one corner of it. "Hope that covers you as well." He stood there a moment as if undecided and suddenly threw out his right hand to Thomas.

Thomas reached to shake, more out of reflex than a conscious decision, but in the act of shaking he shook his head, gripping Pete's hand tightly. "No," he said. "Listen, I need to tell you something. Please. If you don't mind…" He trailed off lamely, nodding at the chair, as Pete slowly sat back down with a puzzled frown on his face.

"Okay. Sure. What is it?"

Quickly, before he could change his mind, Thomas blurted, "I'm as guilty as you were. Guiltier. It was all my fault."

Pete frowned and cocked his head to one side. Just then the waitress stopped at the table. "Wanna 'nother?" she drawled, giving Pete a close once over and liking what she saw.

He nodded and cocked an eyebrow at Thomas. Thomas slid his wet glass across the table, and she took the empties over to the bar for a refill.

"I'm not sure I understand, kid." Pete said after she'd brought fresh refills.

Thomas took a deep breath. "I was forbidden to ride down that hill. My dad and mom always said how dangerous it was. Joel claimed he'd done it once before." Thomas swallowed, couldn't, and sipped some cold soda from the glass, wishing it could dissolve the lump in his throat and the stone lodged like a chunk of ice in his stomach. Was he finally going to release his burden? With this man of all people? He gazed thoughtfully at his hands, curled around the cold glass of dark liquid, beads of water running down the outside, pearling on his fingers. He raised his eyes back to meet Pete's.

"I double dared him," He burst out quickly, harshly, his voice barely above a whisper.

"Say again?" Pete looked quizzical, head cocked to the side, giving a small shake. "I didn't follow that," he added.

Thomas sighed, suddenly realizing how tense he was. Every muscle was tight, like a spring wound to its furthest point. He made himself relax and then continued. "I double dared Joel that morning. If I hadn't, maybe he wouldn't have…" Thomas shrugged, not sure how to continue but desperately wanting Pete to understand.

Pete returned his gaze, face unreadable, still.

Thomas swallowed and lowered his gaze. "If I hadn't dared him like that, maybe he wouldn't have gone. Maybe it would have been me…maybe not. Maybe we both would have turned away. I guess I'll never know. It can't be changed now." He looked back up at Pete and then plunged on. "It wasn't your fault. It was my fault."

The relief that flooded through Thomas was almost overwhelming. It was a feeling equivalent to the greatest joy, the greatest sorrow, the most extreme fear that he'd ever experienced before in his life, all jumbled together, leaving him feeling weak and drained.

Pete met his gaze for a few moments and then nodded gravely. "Dude," he said intently, "I've done my time in prison. I took your friends life that morning. I didn't mean to and I don't think it would have made any difference at all if I hadn't smoked dope. I would have hit him no matter what. There was no way I could have avoided it. I might have stopped. That's absolutely the only difference. I might have stopped. I've done eight years in the pen for that and I deserved every day of it in my opinion. I've served my time." He paused and Thomas felt his gaze locked by the intensity of Pete's stare. "You've done your time, too, man. You need to put this behind you and live your life. It will eat you alive if you don't."

The two men sat in silence until Pete suddenly stood up and held out his right hand. Thomas rose, facing him calmly and grasped Pete's hand in his own. "Thank you," Thomas said, shaking firmly. "Thank you, Pete."

Pete flashed a smile. "You remember what I said now…you let it go." Thomas watched until the door closed, blocking Pete's retreating figure from sight.

RED SKY AT DAWN

Several things occurred suddenly and simultaneously as the elderly lady quickly regained consciousness. Firstly, she was immediately aware the plane was descending much too steeply and swiftly and early to be arriving at their destination. Secondly, once her mind accepted this fact her bladder decided to release its contents in the sudden terror that gripped her. She had heard of the fight or flight syndrome but never having experienced it prior was taken by surprise when it happened to her. Were it not for the seatbelt holding her securely in the seat surely, she would have borne wings and out-flown the very plane itself! Almost immediately after her bladder released, the third and truly shocking thing was her immediate sense of shame. This was discarded almost as quickly as it occurred to her. Because, truly, who would ever know?

Perhaps, she reasoned to herself, they were not crashing after all. Oddly there seemed to be no sound whatsoever in the cabin of the plane. Yet her eyes did not fail her. She could clearly see the other passengers and by the expressions on their faces something must be awry. A quick glance at the pale face of the young woman in the seat next to hers was confirmation. She saw her own terror peering back at her from the deep brown depths. *To think*, she thought, *mine are the last eyes to look into hers and hers into mine.*

The sunlight filling the cabin seemed to be oddly out of place as well. A person just didn't expect to see sunshine...and such bright sunshine...in their final moments. And why was her life not flashing before her eyes? Wasn't that what was supposed to be happening? Instead, she was filled with a sense of loss for what she would miss. Would tomorrow's sunrise be tenderly yellow and golden with touches of pink in a robin's egg blue sky? Or would it be filled with massive thunderheads that would release their bellyful of rain somewhere in the vast distances in the east? She recalled a phrase her grandmother had been fond of saying.

23

Red skies at dawn
Sailors be warned;
Red skies at night
Sailors delight.

Strange to think of her grandmother now. It had been fifty years since she passed. More than half a lifetime ago. Yet the vision of her was as clear in her mind's eye as if it had been only yesterday.

Her heart suddenly hurt. Not the hurt of physical pain but of emotional pain...of monumental, irredeemable loss. To never see another sunrise or sunset. To never hear her son's voice or the dulcet tones of her granddaughter. Ah, now there was a precious and cherished memory to focus on. Her granddaughter was now a young woman, no longer a child, and what a beautiful woman she was developing into. She sang so beautifully, and it was almost an established fact that she would be hugely successful. It was so unfair that she would miss what was surely her crowning achievement.

This thought was running simultaneously with the oddly separate version of herself that was standing by and coldly, analytically, evaluating what was occurring to and around her. The vast discomfort of her now wet clothing. The ironic thought, *Thank God we aren't landing in water. I surely could not use the seat cushion as a floatation device now!* And how could she laugh at a time like this? And yet, a brief chuckle was indeed startled out of her by the immensely funny thought. *I must be in shock,* that coldly separate analyst thought.

This allowed her to focus once again on her aching heart and she recalled a show she had once seen about the mysteries of a broken heart and heartache. Doctors had discovered and it was now an accepted fact that in times of intense sorrow the heart truly did become elongated in the chest cavity and as a result it "ached". Prolonged conditions had even led to death. *Perhaps I can die before we reach the site of the accident,* the lady thought to herself, surprising herself with another little chuckle.

She again glanced at the young woman next to her who was now looking at her oddly. *And no wonder,* she thought. *Who laughs while the plane they are riding on is crashing?* The smile she gave the young woman was no doubt incongruous but at this moment who cared? The young woman's eyes opened even wider...and really, who would have thought it possible? Her body language spoke with even greater clarity as she leaned as far from the older woman as space and seating restrictions would allow.

The older woman turned her eyes away so she could look once again at the visions in her head. No, her life was not flashing before her, but many people were. She had always eschewed much human companionship. Of course, there was her husband and her mind settled gladly on the image of him. Ah, it was their wedding day. He had looked so handsome in his dark suit with the gaily patterned tie. The image of the tie made her fingers itch to reach out and run them lightly under his collar and back under the light fall of his hair that he allowed to grow just over the collar of his shirt yet trimmed neatly enough to not reach beyond to the edge of the folded over collar. That hair in her memory was almost honey in color…not the white it became later.

She had always hoped to be the one to go first but fate had not been so kind. If there was anything about the current situation that she found pleasure in it was the possibility that perhaps, if what they were raised to believe were true, she may indeed be reunited with him at last. The last eleven years without him had been the longest of her life. He had been such a good man…patient and kind, slow to anger and quick to laugh, with an unlimited capacity for love. He had been her perfect foil. How fast the years they were together had flown! Thirty-six years passing in the mere wink of an eye or, so it had seemed.

Perhaps as was only fitting the image of her husband was suddenly superseded by an image of her father. *So finally, we get to the heart of it all*, was her unbidden thought. The one unresolved aspect that had haunted her adult life arose before her and the pain in her heart increased even more. Unbidden and unknown the tears were streaming from her eyes, corneas yellowed from age and clouded with the beginnings of cataracts. The tears made her vision crystal clear. Her father was the young man he had been when she left home. And his image was as unreachable now as it had been in real life.

There was no warmth in the eyes that were a mirror of her own. No smile touched the perfectly molded mouth. Had she loved him so greatly all these years? Had all this love been stuffed hidden down inside without her knowledge? How could it be possible? How could this pain suddenly be so tremendously great and overwhelming? Of all the things she knew she would miss…her granddaughters assured success, the beautiful sunrises and sunsets, the blinding sparkle of the sun on a newly formed icicle as the first morning light catches it hanging from the eaves of the house on Christmas morning…none of it compared to the tremendous loss she still felt for her father.

It surprised her now at her advanced age of eighty to discover that the young child she had been still was. Less than thirty years ago she had helped to lay her father to rest. Not that he laid anywhere. His wishes had been to leave no trace…no written homages, no lengthy sermons from some pulpit that he would not have graced while living, no marker for future generations to know that he had ever existed. Suddenly, as the plane hurtled to the hard ground below, she understood and regretted what he had taken from them…as he had always taken…and the fact that she had been a willing participant. She felt a surprising surge of bitterness and anger. All these years…and the years before that…she had been seeking him yet never finding. And she finally understood that even in his death he had managed to deny the only thing she had ever desired…the chance to tell him the innermost workings of her heart and to receive his blessing and love. There was no gravesite to visit or bring flowers. He would have shunned them while living and succeeded in even repudiating them once dead. And now, as it were, she would follow firmly in the path he had laid before her. She felt keenly the rejection she had felt when she was a young child. No, the man she had sought then and the man he became that she never knew, succeeded in eluding her. She had been a willing assistant in the scattering of his ashes. She had done her share with her sister by her side.

Her analytical double sneered at her. *Typical that you should waste your last thoughts on him. You can rest assured his last thoughts were not of you.*

But was that strictly true?

They had been surprised, her sister and herself, to discover hidden among his personal items small mementoes of their own childhood. What had he been thinking when he kept them? And there was no question that it was him that had done the keeping…and not their mother. Several of the items were hidden where even their mother had not known nor expected to find them. Her sister's cherished mirror that they had long since forgotten but upon finding was as naturally accepted and immediately recognizable as a family portrait. Some of their childhood toys, abandoned in their individual mad flights from the nest.

Neither her sister nor herself had left home on especially gracious or friendly terms. In fact, it was fair to say, both had dashed away as if the devil were chasing and they were in fear of their lives…which they in fact were. But years allowed the memories to fade…never vanish entirely, sometimes popping up vividly when least expected – or desired…but the frequency lessening with time.

She had reached a point where she held imaginary conversations with both of her parents. She would tell them about her home, her life, their great-grandchild and the generations in between during her drive to town. In her late forties the thought occurred one day that perhaps they were no more. The time elapsed so great, almost insurmountable, that who was there to even know she existed that would know how to contact her should anything happen? And then it *had* happened. The phone had rung as she was drifting into sleep one night.

They had flown to their mother's side immediately. The reunion as natural as though the decades intervening had not passed but in one single night. She had cried, yes. She understood later that those tears were more for the loss of the years never to be recovered with the woman she recognized in her heart as her mother. No amount of late-night talks would ever allow them to fully grasp the nuances of the years apart. For that she mourned. Deeply and painfully and she could not bridge that chasm, did not know where to start. The fact that she loved deeply and intensely was never doubted but her conversations did not come easily. She had never been a phone talker, it felt awkward and unnatural to talk to a device and not to a person. For her, body language and expression were as much a part of the conversation as were the words and tone of voice.

But she never truly mourned her father. Or so she had thought and staunchly claimed. She recalled a conversation with her closest friend shortly after he passed and she had told her friend she had not cried for him, did not miss him – how could you miss something you didn't have anyway? Her friend had reassured her, telling her many people did not actually mourn until much later – that one day it would hit her.

"No." She had slowly but firmly shaken her head. "No. I will never mourn him." And she had been true to her word. Or had she been? Now, looking back, she saw and recalled the times of indelible sadness that had consumed her. No apparent cause, just extremely sorrowful.

Her father had been a stubborn man and she resembled him in many regards. Now she finally understood that she had been grieving him all her life. Not just at the scattering of his ashes but instead to the very day she had walked away. That had been the day he had truly died for her. It had taken almost four decades for the physical fact to occur, but she had been grieving the loss of her father for almost sixty-five years and been in a state of denial the entire time. And simple recognition of this basic fact filled her with sudden joy.

Her greatest concern had always been whether he had in fact loved her, felt any pride in her. Her many successes had been her path to self-appreciation. With time and success her sense of self-worth had grown, and she came to love the person she was. She had strong beliefs and she did not compromise. The very qualities she had admired most in her father. And she understood that if she could love herself, he would have as well. If she could admire the woman she had grown into, if she had found peace and serenity in the world she had established, by the fact of their very similarity he could not have helped but feel as she did.

In this last moment as the end rushed to meet her this simple fact filled her suddenly with a comforting warmth. She relaxed into her seat, a smile softly settling on her mouth. She felt peace beyond anything she had ever felt in her life before this, her final moment. *Yes*, she thought, *I am prepared to meet my Father.*

A MODERN FABLE

There were two men who lived in the suburbs and worked in the city. Their lives were similar in many ways. Both had lovely families, nice homes and both men pursued the same line of work, working for the same employer.

One morning the boss called both men and told them that he had a promotion and pay raise he could give to one of them, but not both. He had decided that in order to fairly grant this boon he would give them a task to complete. They would have until the end of that day to complete this task. Now, both men desired the promotion and the pay raise very much but the task the boss had set was very hard and not easy to perform.

The first man struggled with the task and found many reasons why he could not complete it. When he saw the boss at lunch break, and the boss asked how he was doing with the task, he was able to spend an hour explaining how the task could not be done.

The second man, meanwhile, did not break for lunch. He applied himself and tried very hard, but he also was no closer to a solution than the first man. When the boss returned from lunch, he went to the second man to see how he was progressing. The second man explained what he had done so far and some ideas he thought he might try next but admitted he had not solved the task yet.

The rest of the day passed quickly and at the end both men came before the boss. The first man did not complete the task. He felt that after explaining the many reasons the task could not be accomplished, he was doing the boss a favor not spending any more time on it and decided to abandon it when they returned from lunch.

The boss turned to the second man and asked how he had done. The second man did not complete the task. He tried very hard throughout the day but found the task to be insurmountable.

The boss awarded the promotion and the pay raise to the second man.

28

RARE COINS

Am I really going to go through with this? I asked myself as I struggled to pull the heavy case out of the dark corner of the closet. It had sat untouched for the two years I'd lived in the apartment and I'd forgotten just how heavy it was. I lugged it across the room and heaved it up onto the bed, snapping the catches that held it shut. Inside were neatly stacked blue hardboard albums. I didn't need to count to know there were fifteen in three stacks of five, snuggled close together in the old suitcase.

I sighed and turned away from the bed, scanning the clothes hanging in the closet. It seemed silly to agonize over what to wear. I'd never been vain and had never really cared what others thought of how I looked but this was perhaps the most important occasion of my adult life. I wanted to present myself as perfectly as possible.

What would he think of the woman I'd become? It had been thirty-three long years since I'd last seen him; half a lifetime. I'd been a girl of fifteen the day I'd walked out the door and never looked back. *Not that he'd made any effort at the time to call me back, either*, I couldn't help thinking bitterly.

Eureka Springs had been too small for me then; too much the small town and all that goes with a small town…everyone knowing everyone and in everyone's business. I could never comprehend how so many could know so much yet really know so very little.

My father had been a well-liked man. He could be extremely charming and seemed to have a magnetism that made him instantly likeable and respected. That he was a hard worker with a firm work ethic was without question. To all outward appearances ours was a stable and happy household.

Appearances, however, can be quite deceiving. At home he was a mean-spirited alcoholic, free with his fists. Nothing ever met his rigid standards of perfection. The frequent physical abuse may have been bearable, but the psychological damage was far worse.

29

I do not recall ever hearing my father say he loved me. No matter how stellar my achievements, in his eyes I was an abysmal failure and an embarrassment. Or at least that is what I believe. I cannot fathom why he hated me so very much. I know I was an unwanted pregnancy. I know he married my mother because of me and I know he was bitterly disappointed that I was a girl and not the son he longed for.

My glance fell again on the open case on the bed. Yes, I could trace much of the hatred and violence to the contents of this suitcase. Well, not *these* actual contents.

It hadn't been just my home life that resembled a hall in hell. Perhaps other children could sense that I was abused…the way a wolf can sense when an animal is weak or sick and target it as prey. Or perhaps it was my above average intelligence. Learning came easily to me and I was always at the top of the list when it came to grades and attendance.

The attendance was also in large part because of my father. A sick day was unthinkable. He had an abhorrence of illness and I learned early to smother my coughs and sniffles in my pillow so he would not hear and heap further abuse on me.

Whatever the reason or cause, my earliest memories of school are of being an outcast and the target of ridicule and bullying. All of which meant there was no escaping even for brief intervals the torture that was my life. Only my mother offered the love I so desperately craved and she could only give that on the sly. My father was much too jealous of her affection to share it with anyone else.

I never ceased trying. It is perhaps one quality of my personality that has been my greatest asset as well as my most fundamental fault. I don't know when to quit. The good grades were an effort to earn my father's love and respect. In the fifth grade I was tested and found to have an IQ of one hundred sixty. This earned me a spot in our school's gifted program. Surely, I was the only child in the state of Arkansas who attended both special education as well as the gifted program. That this was never a clue to my school teachers that something might be awry can only be an example of the blinders most adults wear when it comes to children. Nor was my father especially impressed with my abilities either.

I tackled the problem of acceptance by trying to buy it. My father had a modest rare coin collection which he kept stored in a bookcase that he'd put in my bedroom when it didn't fit in the living room of the house. We'd moved into the house when I was eight years old. The bookcase had been in the living room of the trailer we lived in previously, but the new house didn't have room for it. Just as I was a castoff, so were the items placed in my bedroom. The rare coin collection was in the bottom of the case behind doors.

My father was of the opinion children should not be seen or heard and so my hours when at home were spent secluded in my bedroom. I was only allowed to come out for meals or to go to school. In good weather I could go outdoors and play in the backyard, but that was the extent and limit of my freedom.

I was a naturally inquisitive child. My intelligence demanded almost constant challenging and I found it in books...but there were times of extreme boredom and one day I decided to explore the contents of the bookcase. It was then that I discovered the coins. As a child I could have no understanding or appreciation of the value of the coins. I knew only that their face value could help me achieve the popularity I craved.

So, I slowly spent most of the coins my father had collected. I'd buy penny and nickel candy at the store I passed on my way to school, filling my pockets with assorted sweets which I would then pass out liberally to my classmates. It never solved my acceptance problem so I learned at an early age that one can't buy affection or friendship. That the children took the candy goes without saying, but it did not stop them from picking on me.

Well, the day finally came when my father decided to pull out his coin collection. Imagine his shock and dreadful rage when he discovered his loss.

I will never forget that day. It was late spring; a rain had freshened the new green growth on the trees and there was a special lovely light and quality to that day that will remain frozen forever in my memory. I sat in my room trembling, knowing what he would find and terrified of the beating I was sure I would receive. That I deserved it was without question in my mind. I had done an awful thing regardless of the logic that impelled me.

The beating never came. I learned from my mother years later that my father was afraid if he did punish me, he might not stop. His rage was so great that he would likely have killed me. It sealed his hatred of me in concrete and from that day forward I was subjected to the cruelest treatment imaginable. I became known as Thief, among other equally hateful titles. Each hurtful word a knife twist in my young heart.

I lived under these conditions until I was fifteen. Then one day something inside snapped and the child would take no more abuse. I did not go home that day. For the remainder of that school year, the spring of my sophomore year in high school, I lived with my closest friend. That my parents never even inquired where I was, never went to the school or the police to investigate my absence, was only a further arrow piercing my fragile heart.

I did not stay with my friend through that summer but determined to put Eureka Springs in my past and close the door forever. I headed south, hitchhiking my way to Dallas. I was heady with freedom and was ready to take the world by storm. I would do big things. My father would hear of my success and regret his treatment of me. I was so naïve. The reality became a hard scrabble existence working as a waitress in a small diner that catered to farmers and ranchers. Tips were adequate but I barely managed to eke out a living.

My years of abuse and unpopularity with my own peers had burdened me with a tremendous inferiority complex. I was never satisfied with my appearance, but I seemed to have inherited my father's magnetism. Men were drawn to me and I discovered the power of my sex. That I used sex to get what I wanted I can say now without shame. I look back and see a sad and lonely young woman still trying to buy her place in the world, trying to buy love and affection...only using my body instead of stolen rare coins. Eventually I learned that men would pay a lot of money to look at my body. I became a stripper at a popular Dallas men's club in my early twenties and it was indeed lucrative.

After a couple of years, I was one of the star attractions at the club, and I was pulling in some serious cash. I had a car of my own, and not some old used clunker either. I had a brand-new car and a nice apartment off Preston...one of the nicer neighborhoods north of Dallas. One evening, while driving to the club, I saw a billboard advertising a coin swap at the Dallas Convention Center. It was billed as the largest rare coin collector swap meet in the South. I suppose it was then the first seed was planted. Perhaps I could still redeem myself. I went to that swap meet and so began my own collection of rare coins. Each previous attempt had failed yet once again I set out to buy that which I most desired...could I *still* buy my father's love? Could I restore what I had taken and win what he had never offered freely?

I shook my head now as I looked at the stack of collector books. The books were full; wheat leaf pennies, buffalo nickels, mercury dimes, silver dollars and more. All the varieties I had pilfered I had managed to collect. This collection far exceeded the modest set my father had started. I recalled he had somewhere between four to five books with pages about half full. I had fifteen completely full.

Stripping had become my second job after I managed to land a position with an insurance company and was starting to earn good money, not to mention benefits and a retirement savings plan with a good match. I didn't need the money from stripping, but it was good. Good cash and I turned all of it into rare coins.

Over the years I resolved my daddy issues. I recognized the psychological satisfaction I was getting from the attention the men in the strip club showered me with and finally I gave it up. I chose the respectable route and very quickly began to climb the corporate ladder. With my excellent memory coupled with my capacity for learning, it was not long before I had reached middle management and was viewed as a successful business woman. The fifteen books of rare coins moved from my bedroom bookshelf. They made their way into the old suitcase and from there to a spot under the bed until I finally buried them in the back of the closet.

I may have been professionally successful, but I was never able to establish a successful partnership. I lived alone with my scared and trembling inner child; the child that still longed for the parental love that all children must crave.

Until one day chance brought me back to Eureka Springs. Some colleagues from work planned a weekend in Branson and I agreed to join them. Knowing I was so close to my old home I extended my stay by a few days and decided I'd take a trip down memory lane.

How to describe the impact when I first came around the bend on highway twenty-three south coming into the north end of town and I spotted the ES&NA Railway with the big engine and the old station house? The old green engine with the Eureka Springs and North Arkansas name proudly stenciled was like an old friend. How the old electric plant husk, draped in choking vines through which the empty eyes of the burned building peered, recalled old delightful tales of hauntings and begged to be explored. Who knew I'd feel such sudden and fierce longing? I was home and my heart almost burst from the joy of it. Thirty-three years had not left much of a mark…everything looked familiar and as they say, only the names had changed.

I drove through the old downtown, past the Auditorium and the gothic courthouse and up Planer Hill. The Queen Anne still perched at the top of Planer Hill in resplendent beauty hinting at the grace of a better day. I knew I would not be able to rest until I'd faced the worst, so I drove back through downtown and followed the historic loop up to The Crescent Hotel. It was still as magical to me today as it had been when I was a child; massive and gothic, mysterious and alluring, cloaked with the secrets of age and history. I followed Kingshighway and took a left onto Singleton feeling every muscle suddenly go tense and jittery. My hands were gripping the steering wheel until the bones of my knuckles showed in white.

Our house had been the fourth on the right and I approached it slowly. I was shocked how dilapidated the two-story house had become. The paint was cracked and peeling, sections of trim rotted and hanging, the front porch steps sagging. The trees and shrubbery had grown wild and threatened to overtake the front door entirely. It was evident the house was deserted, and no one lived there any longer. I pulled into the short drive next to the house, looking up at the windows of the southwest corner, second floor room. That had been my bedroom. I'd spent many a lonely hour gazing out that window towards Kingshighway, dreaming of the day I'd be free from tyranny and terror.

As I got out of the rental car I paused uncertainly. The house itself could give me no answers. My gaze swept the house next door and across the street. I noticed an elderly gentleman doing yard work. I crossed and approached him, not certain how to begin.

"Sir," I fumbled awkwardly, "I wonder if I could ask you a question."

He sat back on his heels, pushing back a worn baseball cap that might once have been blue but was now an indiscriminate shade of dirty gray from his wrinkled forehead. Blue eyes twinkled from under bushy white eyebrows. And then it struck me.

"Mr. Childerness?" I gasped and was rewarded when the eyebrows shot up and surprise leapt into those vivid blue eyes. I remembered those eyes clearly from my childhood.

Mr. Childerness had always been kind to me, handing me a cookie his wife had baked or a piece of candy when I was small, ribbons and once a lovely pair of gloves as I grew older. I had always suspected that the kindness he showed me was his small recompense for the violence he must certainly have overheard.

"My goodness, Mr. Childerness, it is so good to see you. I'm Amy Pardue from across the street." I gestured back at the house looming behind us.

"Well and so you are!" he exclaimed, rising to his feet and roughly, awkwardly patting my shoulder. "How long has it been Amy?" His forehead wrinkled in thought as his eyes drilled into mine.

"Thirty plus years." I confessed.

He shook his head. "Such a very long time. What brings you back?"

I turned and my eyes again scanned the empty edifice looming menacingly in its abandoned state. "I'm not sure." As honest an answer as I could return. "Do you know what became of…" I was unable to finish the sentence and it trailed off into an uncomfortable silence as I turned back to him.

"Well, Miss Amy, I don't wish to be the one to deliver bad news to you, now."

I shook my head. "It's all right, Mr. Childerness. I've longed suspected."

"Your pop lives in Brighton Ridge these days." His hand indicated the house. "It's been empty now…oh, I'm guessing these five years past now." He squinted and looked to the clouds floating in the blue sky as if the answer were written there. "Yep. Been five years October. Shortly after your ma passed." The eyes settled again on mine. "Did you know your ma passed, then?"

Shockingly the tears surfaced swiftly and painfully, my vision crackling into prisms through the unshed moisture and I was unable to speak past the lump that suddenly filled my throat. In the next minute the wiry thin arms had embraced me and rocked me gently as I found myself sobbing on his shoulder, my tears darkening the blue of his coarse denim shirt.

"There now. I know that comes as a blow to you, girl."

I pulled away from him, digging in my shoulder bag for a tissue to dry my streaming eyes and blow my runny nose. "How?"

"Heart failure, I believe it was." He half shrugged, looking away.

I nodded and murmured, "Thank you, Mr. Childerness. It's been so good to see you but I think I'll be running along now."

He nodded and said, "It's mighty good to see you, too, Miss Amy. So many folks have left, so many new folks around…well, it does my heart good to see you."

I didn't stay that night in Eureka Springs as I had planned. I headed back to Missouri and got a room in Branson, just beginning the process of grieving for my mother. But Eureka Springs had set its hooks in me and I could not get it out of my mind. It occurred to me later, after I returned to Dallas, that there was really nothing I wanted more than to return to my roots.

In a chance conversation with my director I mentioned I'd been thinking of a move back to northwest Arkansas some day and one spring afternoon, completely unexpectedly, he called to advise that he was perfectly okay with me making a move. There was absolutely no reason I couldn't perform my responsibilities from there just as easily as I did in Dallas. I was largely working out of my apartment already anyway.

I immediately began my search for living quarters and six months later made my move back to Eureka Springs, having acquired a spacious apartment on Armstrong. And now, almost two years later, I was finally determined to see my father and resolve our differences…or at least make the attempt.

I settled on a simple black skirt suit with a plain white blouse and modest black pumps, pulling my hair into a ponytail and applying a minimum of makeup. My father had never approved of overly made up women. I was finally as ready as I thought I would ever be and I lugged the heavy case down to my car.

The distance from my apartment on Armstrong to Brighton Ridge was no more than a couple of miles and I was there within a matter of minutes. I sat in the car for a moment trying to calm myself. Just as I had reacted the first time I drove down Singleton I was reacting now to the prospect of walking through those doors and confronting the man that had loomed so largely my entire life. My stomach was a knot…I felt like I needed to burp or throw up. My hands were shaking when I pulled them away from their death grip on the steering wheel. A glance in the visor mirror made me wish I'd applied a little more makeup when I saw the pale and scared face staring back at me. For a minute I imagined turning the key and driving back to my apartment, let this madness go.

Rather than succumb to that temptation I opened my door and stepped out into the warmth of the summer day, hauling the heavy suitcase from the back seat. A middle-aged woman with frizzy yellow hair and sharp blue eyes magnified behind thick lenses looked at me quizzically as I approached across the lobby. It was tastefully decorated but still had that antiseptic smell and feel that you typically associate with hospitals. Everything was hushed and quiet like a library. "You have a Mr. Pardue here, I believe?" I asked in answer to the unspoken question in those cerulean eyes.

She turned to the computer monitor angled in a corner of her desk and I could see her typing the name in. "No Perdue, here, no, ma'am."

"Not Perdue. It's Pardue. P-A-R-D-U-E. His first name is Henry."

She pursed her lips a bit, I suppose in disapproval of my not giving her the spelling the first time, and typed a bit more. "And your relationship to Mr. Pardue?" Again, with the piercing, suspicious stare.

"I'm his daughter."

"Oh!" She looked at her screen and frowned. "There is no next of kin listed, no daughter mentioned." She looked at me again.

I had anticipated that this might happen and I was prepared. I pulled an envelope from my purse and handed her my birth certificate. "Perhaps this will establish my relationship?"

She accepted the document and looked it over carefully and then looked back at me. "One moment please."

She turned and picked up the phone on the other corner of her desk and I heard her say, "Someone is here to see Mr. Pardue. Claims she's his daughter and has a birth certificate. It has Henry Pardue listed as her father and the signature looks pretty similar to the one in his record." She paused and I could tell she was listening. Finally, she said, "Okay, thank you," and set the handset back in its cradle.

"If you'll wait right over there, someone will be out in just a minute." She indicated a bench on the opposite wall with a tilt of her frizzy head.

I was too nervous to sit so instead I studied the bulletin board posted on the wall next to the front door. I don't remember a single item that was posted on that board. My mind was racing, my heart pounding. *I'm really doing this. I am really going to follow through on this.*

Behind me someone cleared their throat and spoke, "Excuse me. Are you looking for Mr. Pardue?"

I swung around to face a youngish man, possibly in his early twenties. "Yes. I'm his daughter. I'd like to see him."

"If you'll follow me, please." He turned and headed down one of the long halls radiating out from the lobby, his shoes squeaking slightly on the highly polished linoleum, my own clacking loudly in my ears. I should have worn quieter shoes.

If I had thought I felt like throwing up in the parking lot it was nothing compared to what was currently happening to my insides. "Sir?" I interrupted my host.

He stopped so suddenly I almost ran into him. "Yes?"

"I wonder if you have a restroom I could use before..." I trailed off uncertainly. Before what? Before facing the father I hadn't seen in three decades? Before I threw up all over their shiny linoleum and made a mess? Before I could turn and run back to the safety of my car?

He seemed to understand. He smiled gently and said, "Of course. There's a public restroom just down the hall here. Not far from your father's room. I'll wait for you."

I went in and realized I did have to use the restroom. I've always seemed to respond to stressful situations by a sudden need to relieve myself. While washing my hands I avoided looking at myself in the mirror. If I confronted the fear, I knew was there I would not have the courage to continue. I could not come all this way and all these years and not seek the resolution I now understood I so desperately craved and needed. Resolutely I retrieved the suitcase and stepped back out into the hallway.

"Ready?" The young man had waited as promised.

I nodded, not able to speak just yet.

"Your father will be right through this door, then." And he flourished his hand towards a door two down from the restroom.

I thanked him and he left me standing there. I was uncertain what to do next. Should I knock? Or just barge in. I could discern no sound on the other side of the door. If there was a television on, the volume was too low to hear. I raised my hand to knock and froze. It didn't feel right. Instead I lowered my hand to the lever of the door handle and slowly forced myself to press it down, feeling the catch retreat from the striker plate as I eased the door open slowly.

The room beyond was dark and shadowy, the curtains drawn to keep out the fierce glare of the afternoon summer sun. I could hear the soft whisper of an air conditioning unit and I felt goosebumps rise on my arms from the artificial chill of the room.

It took a moment for my eyes to adjust to the gloom. The room was small and like a hospital room. A small bathroom opened off to the left with the main room opening out from a small entryway. The bed was against the wall to the left, a television mounted in the corner opposite with a couple of chairs grouped under it.

In the center of the bed a white-haired man sat reading a magazine. I couldn't tell which magazine because he held it folded over to the page he was reading. He was dressed in a white t-shirt and pajama bottoms, horned feet with yellowed nails appending below the pajama legs. A white sheet was pulled partially across his lap, the rest rumpled and twisted to one side. His nails needed trimmed and I felt a pang of pity for the husk of the man I saw before me.

At first, I didn't believe I had the right room. "I'm sorry. Please excuse me."

I turned to leave but the man had lifted his head and pinned me with his eyes. Eyes I knew instantly. Eyes I had forgotten that I remembered so well. My father's eyes. Something happened in my chest, I felt my heart slam against my rib cage and I staggered a step, the suitcase seeming to pull me.

As I stumbled, he half-struggled to rise. "No," I managed to choke, holding up my free hand in a gesture to stay. "I'm...I'm okay." I set the suitcase down and smoothed my suit. And then we just looked at each other.

His look was puzzled. "Can I help you with something?" he asked.

I felt an insane urge to laugh. *Help me? Oh yes...oh yes you could help me. You could help me understand so much.* But I didn't say it and mercifully I did not laugh. I also realized I had no idea what to say. None. I was completely speechless.

"Miss? Are you okay?" he asked, leaning forward, causing the pillow propped behind his back to slide down behind him, his hand starting to reach for the nurses call button on the handrail of the raised upper half of his bed.

He looked so unbelievably frail and old lying in that bed and I suddenly felt incredibly foolish. What was I doing? Why had I done this? "Daddy?" It was the only thing I could think to say. It came out in a whisper and I don't think he even heard me.

"Miss?" he prompted again.

I cleared my throat and spoke louder, "Daddy, it's me. It's Amy."

For a moment he froze, the hand poised over the call button trembling in the air before dropping back into his lap, struggling to lean back...the slipped pillow preventing him. I reacted, stepping to his side and pulling the pillow back into position so he could lean back. He did, his rheumy eyes never leaving mine, breath rasping harshly in his thin chest. I retreated a step, placing distance between us.

I could feel my insides churning, a toxic mix forming in my stomach that threatened to erupt. I tried swallowing but there was no saliva in my mouth to wash past the sudden dryness in the back of my throat. I heard my tongue click against the arid roof of my mouth and it sounded like an explosion to my ears. I could feel my muscles beginning to tremble. To still the physical reaction, and to stifle my overwhelming sense of panic, I grasped my hands firmly together, clenching tightly, focusing and trying to still my racing heart.

"Amy?" He looked puzzled, the word was spoken as if in a foreign language and unfamiliar to him, the word not striking comprehension.

My heart sank. *Did he not even remember me? His own daughter?* A great weakness seized me then and my knees no longer had the strength to support me. I stumbled to the end of the bed, slumping into one of the hard vinyl chairs.

We gazed at one another for a long moment and then he repeated, "Amy." This time it came out more as a sigh of wonder and a new and different feeling crept into my heart. "Is it really you? After all this time," his voice faded on the last word.

No words came to me, as I sat and stared mutely at him. The moment dragged on and he struggled to sit straighter in the bed, fumbling awkwardly behind his back. I half rose to help and he waved his hand brusquely, shaking his head. "Don't need your help." The words were gruff, rumbling out. Suddenly I felt awash in pity for this proud man, struggling now just to sit erect.

"I know you don't," I replied, quietly, and watched him settle back, our eyes again meeting and locking.

"You look well," he said, his manner grudging.

I smiled awkwardly, "Thanks. Are you comfortable?" I asked.

He sighed, and his gaze swept the room. I looked around and saw now how dismal it looked. There were no signs of personal effects, no flowers, no cards…the room was barren and sterile, antiseptic like a hospital room. I could smell the faint odor of bleach used to wash the scuffed linoleum tiles and saw the tiny nap on the thin sheet ending above my father's bony ankle. How dreadful must it be to live in this room day after day, I wondered bleakly. My heart swelled with pity. My gaze finally came to rest on the suitcase standing at the foot of the bed where I had set it down.

"I'm glad you came."

The words startled me, and I tore my gaze from the suitcase back to the man before me. I was shocked to see tears forming in those once brilliant eyes. Of all the scenarios I'd played out in my mind this had not been one of them. The tears spilled over and he reached up to remove his glasses, wiping angrily at the wet tracks on his cheeks. He fumbled out for the box of tissues on his night stand, but it was just beyond his reach. I rose quickly and retrieved them, putting the box in his hand. He nodded gratefully and took a tissue, wiping at his eyes.

The silence lengthened, and I heard the air conditioner tick and then fire in the stillness, the rush of forced air filling the room with white noise. Somewhere in the room a clock was ticking loudly, and I finally traced it to the large round clock on the bathroom wall diagonal to the industrial sink with metal counter space. A lone toothbrush to clean dentures leaned crookedly from a clear plastic cup next to a blue plastic denture container, a box of denture cleaning tablets standing beside them. Next to these items lay a small red comb and a brown brush with strands of white hair and lint caught in the bristles. A walker was positioned between the sink and the bed.

I looked back at my father and was instantly uncomfortable with the intense way he stared at me. "I'm glad," he repeated.

I nodded. "I've wanted to come for some time." The words came out thick and choked. I cleared my throat.

"Water?" he offered.

I nodded gratefully and rose to retrieve a paper cup from the dispenser over the sink. He struggled with the pitcher and I said, "Here, let me." I waited for him to pull his hand away and then poured some of the cold water into the paper cup.

"Would you like some?" I asked. He nodded, tapping his hand next to a clear plastic cup on the tray stand angled next to his bed, where he had laid his magazine. I filled his cup, returned the pitcher to its place on the stand,

and returned to my seat.

We both drank in silence, while I studied the pattern of shadows on the wall from the closed curtains. Somewhere outside came the drone of a motor, a leaf blower perhaps or a weed eater. It was such an ordinary sound and a reminder of the external world. I realized how tense I was. I forced myself to relax. "Are you in any discomfort?" I asked, not sure, now that I was here, what to do.

He shook his head. "No more than normal."

When I looked at him quizzically, he gave a sarcastic laugh that was so much like the father I remembered that I couldn't help but smile, just a little, in response. "Old age," he snorted. "Not for the weak, let me tell you."

I smiled in what I hoped was a commiserate manner. Silence descended again and this time I met his gaze squarely and he was the first to look away.

He started to speak, "Your mother..." but then his voice trailed off again. He cleared his throat and drank some more of the water. "She's passed, you know?" He tried to say it matter-of-factly, but I heard the slight question, the doubt and query, in his tone of voice.

I looked away now at the dull lime green linoleum flooring, the large wheel at the foot of the corner of the bed, dust and hair caught in the wheel assembly. I nodded. "Yes. I know." My voice surprisingly strong and firm.

"It was a heart attack," he said.

More silence, the clock ticking loudly, maddeningly, in the stillness of the room. The drone outside had ceased, it was as if the outer world had also ended. All that remained was this moment in this room.

I nodded finally, accepting the simplicity of the statement. "I have missed her," I said quietly, looking back at him, searching his face and seeing a fresh flow of tears coursing down the wrinkled cheeks.

"I miss her, so God damned terribly!" The fierceness with which he said it shocked me. "There's not a day..."

I saw then that he was grasping something in his left hand, a small square of metal. Suddenly, recognition, as I realized it was a small frame. He held it now, cradled in his lap, his eyes fixed. I could not resist temptation. Rising, I went to his side so I could see what he held. Tears flooded my eyes, my throat constricted, and a lance of pain tore through my chest as I gazed down at my mother's lovely face. She had been such a beautiful, graceful woman and the picture portrayed her memory perfectly. I was sitting in her lap, smiling into the camera. I appeared to be about five years old in the picture.

"Such a beautiful family. I was so proud." A horned and cracked, yellowed thumb brushed lovingly across the surface of the glass.

I leaned a hand on the edge of the bed for a moment to steady myself, not sure I had the strength to remain, but also not confident I could make it back to the chair. I wanted nothing more than to just fold myself into a small ball on the floor, wrapping my arms around myself until the pain passed. I could not believe how incredibly intense my feeling of loss and grief was.

Suddenly my wrist was clasped in a vicelike grip. "She loved you!" He spoke in a low tone but with strength and resolve. "She loved you and never stopped loving you."

I lifted my eyes to his, expecting to see anger and condemnation. Instead I saw an incredible need for understanding, his eyes pleading with mine. I nodded as the tears spilled over and I brushed them away, my fingers pressing against my lips, wanting to dam up the words that struggled to come out, unable to hold them back. "I know that. God, how I know that. And I have loved you both!" It came out before I could stop it. I stared at him, stricken.

And incredibly, his face broke into a smile of joy. "Oh, Amy! Oh, my sweet girl! I never hoped to hear…" and the next moment I had thrown my arms around his neck and he held me tightly, so tightly.

My visit that day was cut short. Shortly after we pulled apart a nurse attendant came in and announced cheerfully that it was time for Mr. Pardue's daily therapy session, and isn't it nice that he has a visitor today?

I agreed to come back and visit with him the next day and it was only later, as I made my solitary dinner, that it occurred to me I'd forgotten all about the suitcase of rare coins. It sat still, at the foot of his bed, as forgotten as the first set.

A MODERN FAIRYTALE

Once upon a time, in 2018 to be exact, there was a young woman named Ella who lived in a dormitory on the campus of Texas Woman's University in Denton, Texas. Ella was a very bright young woman preparing to graduate *Magna Cum Laude* Bachelor of Arts with a double major in English Lit and History. Ella's future was all mapped out, thanks to her loving parents, and she had confidence in her future. She would go on to a doctorate degree, probably in English, and then become a professor…or possibly a teacher. Perhaps one day Ella would think about Ella and what Ella wanted but that was for another day.

On this bright spring day, Ella was packing for Spring Break. She was excited at the prospect. She had worked hard in her senior year and was ready for some time to herself. The campus was abuzz with the excited plans of her fellow seniors. Like locusts, they would descend down the eastern seaboard, flooding the cities with their youthful exuberance, squandering money none of them had, flaunting their youth and sensuality, and ultimately earning the scorn of those that lived in these dens. This was not for Ella. No, Ella planned to escape.

Ella shrugged into her flannel shirt and left it hanging loosely over her jeans and sneakers. Her silky blond hair was pulled into a casual ponytail swinging down her back. She swept her gaze around the room and spotted the thin stack of papers left on her desk. Ella was almost, but not quite, a neat freak and frowned now seeing the papers laying there. Crossing she picked them up and sighed as she scanned the first page. It was a good story. They were getting better with time.

She shuffled the papers neatly together and carried them to her closet. At the back, in the left corner, sat a box. The box was about twelve inches tall and twelve inches wide and had held two thousand five hundred sheets of paper. It, along with the four-in-one printer, had been a gift when she started college four years ago. The paper had been removed a long time ago and unbelievably she had used it all and needed more. The box was now home to a stack of neatly typed, and ignored, stories.

Ella dropped this latest addition on top of the pile, noticing the box was almost a third full. This, too, was four years of work.

No, not work, Ella thought…mere play. Dreams and events, dramas and romances. Ella put the lid back on the box, and on her dreams, and returned to reality.

There! The room was neat, and she was ready to begin her Spring Break. With a spring in her step, Ella swung her overnight bag to her shoulder, locked the door behind her, and so began her adventure.

Ella had rented a remote campsite on a beautiful lake in northwest Arkansas, a short six-hour drive from campus yet an entirely different world. It was the ideal immersion into nature that Ella felt she needed to recharge her drained batteries.

The next morning. she awoke with first light and was enchanted by the tendrils of mist rising from the smooth surface of the still waters of the lake, pewter gray in the early light. She emerged from the tent and stirred awake the coals of the previous night's fire, feeding small sticks into the warmly glowing heart of the coalbed. Before long a weak but steady flame had grown, and she laid on some larger limbs while she attended to breakfast. A short while later, water boiling she made her bowl of instant oatmeal and cup of instant coffee, wincing at the bitterness of the latter while enjoying the creamy goodness of the first.

She had the campground to herself on this Saturday morning in late March. There had been a brief shower during the night and the morning was full of the sound of dripping water on the leaf strewn forest floor, the rustle of leaves as small animals and birds rooted under the leaves for their breakfast.

As Ella enjoyed her second cup of coffee, she felt her muse calling. Pulling a well-worn brown journal from her backpack she bent and wrote, fully absorbed, for the next forty-five minutes while the sun crept up the sky. Finally, she reached for the cup, wincing at the awful taste of the now tepid instant coffee, a thick murk lurking at the bottom of the blue tin cup.

Ella tucked the new story tenderly away, pleased with her morning work. If only this could *be* her work, she thought wistfully. She had no driving desire or passion to be a teacher. She remembered now the praise her creative writing teacher had lavished on her.

"You're the first real talent I've seen since I started teaching!" she'd declared when she'd had a private conference with Ella. "You really need to pursue your gift. You could be the next big thing in writing."

Ella also recalled her mother's response when she'd proudly told her about it.

Her mother had snorted in distain, blowing on her still damp fingernails, "Easy for a teacher to say," she'd replied smartly and then looked at Ella. "If there was any profit in it then why isn't she doing it herself?"

Ella had found the argument a hard one to defend. The statistics were all too clear: very few authors succeeded to the extent they could support themselves on a writing income. Most took secondary jobs to the craft becoming journalists, teachers, advertising scripters…there was a long list where frustrated artists could hide their desires and make a successful living in the eyes of the world. Ella accepted this as her destiny, too.

She heated a second pot of water and made a thermos of hot cocoa, tucking it into her backpack and checking that she had her camera, her journal, some pens, a few granola bars and two bottles of water.

Everything in place, Ella slung the backpack over her shoulder and struck off on the winding trail that led away eastward into the forest, following the line of the shore. The path wound through the trunks of tall pines, tops swaying in a gentle breeze not felt at the lower level, the lake glimmering off to her right. She walked for about an hour, the path easy and carpeted with old pine needles, sun gleaming fitfully through the leafy tree canopy. Rock outcroppings and bluffs snugged up on her left and she delighted in the squirrels scampering through the brush, dense in places. At one point a large tree had fallen across the path and Ella could either find a way through the surrounding foliage or scramble over the mossy trunk. She chose to skirt the massive hulk and was rewarded by the glimpse of a large rock hugged tightly by the ball of the roots. A bright vein of crystal shot the morning sun into prismatic rays briefly blinding her. She gasped in wonder and peered at the rock forever wedded to the long dead tree.

After a while the path emptied into a small glade. A gentle stream split the small meadow in two, a slight waterfall spilling over into the blue lake beyond. Several tall and stately trees with large boles provided shelter and prevented ground cover from overwhelming the gentle slope above which boulders thrust up towards a blue sky. A narrow ravine wound up to the north, allowing egress to higher ground. Ella could see where an apparent natural spring spilled out of a naturally carved rock spillway and formed the stream. Someone had built a rough but sturdy bridge across the stream, using logs at each end as anchor and support.

Ella crossed the bridge and discovered a lovely ledge just made for sitting back and enjoying the serenity of this secluded spot. She set aside her backpack, poured a capful of the cocoa and smiled contentedly as she studied the peaceful vale.

Moss grew in a thick carpet at the base of the ancient hardwoods rising beside the stately, slender pines with their densely needled tops looking like fur against the blue sky. Limestone bluffs gleamed whitely through dense mats of mossy green; wild, delicate ferns clinging in small crevasses. A patch of deep purple and gold caught Ella's eye and she was delighted to spy a patch of wild violas growing thickly at the edge of the stream. As she studied the microcosm at her feet more and more tiny wild flowers sprang to notice…light lavenders, a deep blue, pure and snowy white. A subtle pink peeked shyly from under the root of an old and gnarled walnut tree, looming impressively above them.

She sat sipping her cocoa, enjoying the sounds of the birds and began to feel a bit sleepy. There was a patch of moss, exposed to the warm midmorning sun that seemed to be calling to her. Ella carried her backpack over, snugging it into a fork of the root and spreading a small plaid blanket over the moss, curled up on her side and was asleep in minutes.

When Ella opened her eyes, the sun had marched across the glade and she rested now in shade, the sun having slipped behind the western edge of the tree canopy. She sat up, groggy with sleep and stretched deeply, arching her back, eyes tightly closed. As her body relaxed from the delicious tension, she opened her eyes, and froze, startled. Everything had changed while she slept! She leapt up; the moss springy beneath her feet. It seemed to stretch like a vast emerald carpet before her. Only this carpet had a nap that came to her ankles. If she was not careful her feet would snag. She glanced hurriedly upward and shrank in fear.

The old walnut tree dwarfed the redwoods in size! Its girth was unimaginable, stretching away to her left and her right!! Craning back as far as she could, so far she stumbled back a full step, it towered over her into a sky of enormity looming far above. She grew dizzy looking up at such vastness and quickly looked back down.

Tentatively, she reached a toe forward into the dense lush matt of the moss. Thin stalks rose around her with heavy droopy heads, weighed down with sparkling drops of dew that glittered brightly. Ella gazed in wonder at her reflection in one of the dangling drops of water, distorted by the teardrop shape making her appear comical and tiny.

Why, that was it! She *was* tiny! She stood in amazement gazing about her. Yes, these were the same trees…just ever so much larger from her suddenly diminutive stature. She needed something to give her some perspective and recalled the clump of violas growing next to the stream. They would serve!

Ella ran across the moss now, heading in the direction she remembered the path to be and skidded to a stop at the edge. The path was now a considerable drop, not the barely noticeable step it had once been. She glanced to her left, and right, and saw that the moss tapered to an easy descent to the path a little farther to her right. Nimbly she skipped across and was shortly on the path.

Pebbles that would have been lost in the rubble of the path were now large rocks and even some that qualified as boulders. Soon the path wound past the crude bridge and curved to the north, disappearing up the ravine towards the source of the water, the spring. Ella gazed in dismay at the crude bridge. She recalled the steep step off as she had crossed. The last truss was laid across a large cedar log that served to brace the two sides of the bridge as well as anchor it in the soft earth. That log now loomed above Ella's head and the bridge truss itself was far out of her reach. She would not be crossing the stream that way.

Her marvel at the situation, however, remained undiminished and she gazed up in wonder as a large shadow crossed over her. She did not glimpse what created the shadow, but her gaze settled on a beautiful vision of blue and black and white. An enormous butterfly! Why, it was easily a third her own size now! She watched as it landed gracefully on a nearby stone outcropping.

"So beautiful!" she exclaimed softly, extending her hand to the gently waving luminescent wing, flashing iridescently in the morning sunlight filtering through the tree canopy high overhead.

The butterfly turned to regard her with an eye that gleamed brightly, a prism reflecting the varied colors of a rainbow. The long proboscis of the tongue extended inquiringly towards Ella, scenting the air to identify this strange creature.

Confused by the scent, associated with the much larger and fearsome being that stalked on two legs, the butterfly launched itself to find a more secluded and less threatening perch. Ella followed the brief flight, watching as the butterfly floated down and out of her sight up near what must be the head of the spring.

Sighing she returned to the path and her progress towards the violas. Coming abreast of them she was amazed to discover she was of an equal height. The scent was overwhelming, and Ella inhaled deeply of the perfume. She brushed her finger across the velvet smoothness of a flower petal, marveling at the leathery texture.

Suddenly she was alerted to a new sound. It sounded like a chainsaw! Ella turned sharply to see what the cause of the noise was and sprang back in sudden fear! A fat yellow and black bee was buzzing furiously just behind her! His legs were covered with large particles of pollen, dusty yellow stuck to the sharp bristles on the shiny black legs. The stinger protruding at the base of the body was truly frightening! Why, if he stung Ella with that it might go completely through her arm or her leg…and surely it would strike through tender internal organs if it stung her stomach or back! Quickly she scrambled to the side, out of the way of the bee, watching as it dipped into the violas to gather more pollen.

Shaking, she dropped to a crouch along the edge of the path, suddenly realizing how terrifying this larger world was. She smiled ruefully. Not so very different from the change she was experiencing leaving college. She would be a very small piece in a very large world. Yet, she could navigate that world.

How much harder still to try to succeed with her real passion? Everyone knew you couldn't make it as an author. It was a silly dream.

She drily reflected that the current situation was a bit ironic. At her normal size, she was confident in her world, if she stayed within the safely defined boundaries. To venture into the unknown, to take the plunge and pursue her creativity, was akin to what she was experiencing in her vastly altered state.

She was plunged again into shadow which just as swiftly passed. Glancing quickly upward she was again unable to glimpse the cause.

Nearby a persistent chattering began. It was a quite annoying chirp that was shrill and insistent, filled with alarm. Looking around to locate the source, Ella spied a chipmunk sitting on the top edge of a protruding rock midway up to the spring. His size was quite alarming, and she recalled how *fast* they were! If he chose to attack her…She looked around wildly, wondering where she could go for safety. There! An old tree hugged the rugged path and at its base was a gnarled tangle of roots that she could squeeze into. She didn't spend too much time considering whether the chipmunk could do the same.

She glanced back at the chipmunk, which sat quietly now cleaning its front paws and studying Ella with an alert eye. She decided that to advance further towards the chipmunk might be considered aggressive. She knew they were very territorial. Glancing about her, she saw the gleam of water off to her left, where the stream gently flowed to the small waterfall into the lake.

Recalling her thirst, Ella struck off through the clumps of marsh grass and the occasional viola, spying more bees collecting the pollen from the vibrant blossoms. She reached the bank of the stream and was delighted to see she could easily reach the water without fear of getting wet. She scooped handfuls, drinking thirstily of the cold, fresh spring water. It tasted so good!

Sitting back, thirst slaked, Ella gazed about her again with wonder and joy at the changed aspect of her world. The small stream she could easily have hopped across was now the size of a small and swiftly flowing river. Crossing was far too hazardous a consideration and she shuddered to think what the consequences would be should she slip and fall into the icy water. She would be carried out into the main body of the lake with little hope of survival.

She tried now to recall what wildlife called this area home. She knew the standard list: chipmunks, squirrels, raccoons, armadillos, opossum, bob cat, fox and deer. Also coyotes not to mention all the types of snakes.

She shuddered now remembering the sign at the campground. Beware of water moccasins, copper heads and timber rattlers…all three were quite common here. A picture of each had been displayed and Ella didn't need a reminder that her reduced size posed a very serious issue if she were to cross paths with one of these fearsome predators.

She ran briskly down the path now, back towards the unscalable bridge. As she ran, the shadow passed over her again, for the third time. This time, Ella heard the thin, high shriek of a bird of prey, and her heart thundered in her chest. She was such a small thing now...surely too small for the bird to bother with.

All the same, Ella felt instinctively that she was in grave danger, and she veered suddenly, diving under an overhanging shelf of rock. She pressed her back tightly to the packed earth, the protruding lip of rock forming a rough ceiling above her.

No sooner had she braced herself, with a resounding thud that seemed to shake the ground, a heavy bird landed not more than two feet from where Ella cowered. She could not see much of the bird without moving from her hiding spot, and she was not willing to do that. Large black and gray, wrinkled legs with wicked long talons at the end of spindly long toes gripped at the surface of the dirt path, digging furrows in the thin dust coating. She thought she saw a flash of white or blue belly.

Ella realized she had been holding her breath and released it carefully now, not wanting to attract the bird's attention. She could all to easily imagine the sharp long beak easily reaching her in her tiny hiding place.

She watched tensely as the bird strutted about, cawing noisily, before finally leaping out of sight. Whether the bird had flown away, or just hopped somewhere out of her line of sight, Ella was not prepared to take any chances and thus remained in her hiding place.

As she cowered there, listening intently to the sounds around her, the afternoon seemed to darken and then she heard a noise that caused her heart to begin racing again. Thunder! Her tiny ears vibrated with the sheer size of the sound and now she began to worry about something else. Water. If it were to rain, was she safe in this spot or might the depression fill with water? She remembered again the tree with the roots overhanging the path. If she could make it there, she might find adequate protection.

Carefully, Ella eased herself to the edge of her hiding place, glancing furtively about. Nothing threatening was within sight, but in her mind, she imagined the bird poised above her on the rock just waiting for her to make an appearance. Boldly, she stepped into the path and turned quickly. There! She turned to the right, crouching defensively, but it was only a fallen branch with a single leaf waving despondently, tricking her into thinking it was a bird ready to pounce!

She turned again, searching now for the tree with the protective roots as another rumble of thunder caused her to press her palms to her ears. Finally, she spotted it and began running towards it. She had not gone five steps before the first spatter of rain fell, missing her on her left by mere inches. The huge droplet burst into a spray that drenched her from her left hip to her ankle. Another drop struck her right shoulder as she reached the roots, launching herself between a gap into the drier space beyond. The drop that had struck Ella on the shoulder had drenched her right side entirely and just as she slipped behind the screen of roots a drop glanced off the back of her head, sending cold tendrils down her back.

She huddled beneath the tree, its massive weight looming darkly above her, trying desperately not to think of the spiders that must have homes up in the rotted underside of the pulpy wood. She turned to survey the area, depressed by the rain and the dark recess where she hid. The earth had eroded quite a distance and she had plenty of room to move about. She found a dry pocket not far from the entrance and sat watching the rain fall until finally it stopped. The forest was quiet, only the occasional spatter of rain dripping from leaves at an errant breeze breaking the stillness.

Ella tentatively returned to the path and hurried back the way she'd come. She was aware that she was very hungry and thought wistfully of the granola bars in her backpack. That was an unrealistic goal and she was resigned to an empty stomach.

She felt incredibly drowsy after the excitement of the morning and she thought yearningly of the soft bed of moss. Nothing seemed better than a nap.

Ella reached the spot and deftly climbed back up to the green spongy surface, creeping quietly up next to the large knotty root of the looming walnut thrusting from the ground. She sat hugging her knees to her chest against the rough wall the root formed.

She reflected on the irony of the situation. She was in the same world she had been in before only she was ever so much smaller. Where she had felt in control and confident before, now she felt overwhelmed and terrified. Things that had barely caught her attention were suddenly threatening. A chipmunk or a bird were fierce foes now.

It would be the same if she were to pursue her dreams and not the safely mapped future in which she was certain to succeed.

Where was the joy in safety? Ella recalled the brief encounter with the butterfly earlier in the day. She had been enraptured with the creature's beauty. Seeing it from a different perspective allowed her to see the whole creature differently and she longed to put her thoughts into words.

She recognized now that only by expressing her words in writing was she able to achieve true happiness. She did not want to be the crystal rock forever married to the dead tree.

She glanced longingly around the sun dappled moss, shining brightly in the late afternoon sunlight. Well, there was nothing she could do now about writing or futures…she had to survive the here and now and figure out her next steps. She smiled wanly as a hunger pang made her stomach groan in protest. Her eyelids felt so heavy. She would just take a nap and then perhaps she could forage for something to eat.

Ella laid over on her side, snug up against the tree root, a bit of sun warming her on her soft bed of moss, and closed her eyes. Within moments she fell into a deep slumber while the sun crept across the sky and dipped into the line of trees on the western edge of the clearing.

She awoke from deep sleep, becoming aware rapidly of her surroundings. Her back ached abominably and she could feel a sharp tree root digging into the soft flesh over her kidneys. She opened her eyes slowly, and as her surroundings came into focus, she gasped and sat up with a start.

She was back to her normal size! The large tree root that had sheltered her, was now what dug painfully into her side. The large expanse of moss was now barely large enough for her to sit on.

Joyously, Ella sprang up and returned to her campsite...and so her adventure ended.

She did not return to graduate school that autumn. Instead, she vastly dismayed her parents when she enrolled in an advanced writing course that summer. Her short story documenting her day of wonder was sold to a large national magazine and Ella's writing career was established.

Ella lived happily ever after.

LIVING DEAD WILL

Clarisse thought her heart would burst from sheer happiness. She took a deep breath of the fresh, crisp air, throwing her head back, and closing her eyes. She felt the first rays of the early morning sun kissing her face, feeling its warmth against her closed eyelids. The mountain valley was filled with the song of birds.

"So much for the peace and quiet of nature!" she said with a small laugh, turning to her husband sitting on the log beside their small campfire.

He laughed and nodded, "Indeed! Though I much prefer these sounds to the ones we hear at home." He sipped from his steaming cup of coffee and patted the log next to him invitingly. "Bring that lovely body over here. I don't think I got a proper good morning kiss."

With a broad smile, Clarisse willingly complied. Snuggling next to him on the log, she cradled the hot cup of coffee he handed her, while exchanging a tender kiss. "I'll clean up the stuff from last night while you fix us breakfast," she offered.

"That sounds like a deal, since all I have to do is heat water." Dale grinned as he pulled two containers of instant oatmeal from his pack.

"That's cheating!" Clarisse chimed good-naturedly, placing the plastic wine glasses and plates from the previous evening's meal in a pan and carrying them over to the icy waters of the clear stream that meandered through the center of the small valley they had camped in.

By the time Clarisse had washed and dried the few items, packing them neatly into her pack, Dale had the steaming bowls of oatmeal ready. He spread their map of Yellowstone out on the log between them and studied it intently while they ate. "We parked at this Ranger Station," he said, pointing at a spot on the map, "And as near as I can tell, this is where we are now."

She looked at the spot he indicated. It was a geological map, showing elevations, and she wasn't as comfortable reading it as she was a normal map.

"If you say so."

Dale chuckled. "I do say so, my lovely wife." He leaned over and kissed her tenderly on the corner of her mouth. "Now, do you think these wolves might be anywhere nearby?"

Clarisse shrugged. "I really don't know. From what I was reading online they could be just over the next ridge...or nowhere near. I was a little disappointed when we didn't hear any last night. That's not a good sign. They tend to talk to one another in the evening."

"Maybe they didn't have anything to say," Dale offered hopefully. "Well, I vote we head up that mountain over there...the one to the east. We'll work our way up. See how this valley sort of rises and extends around to the northeast?" His finger trailed between concentric circles on his map. "I think if we follow that trailhead we saw yesterday evening, it goes up that ridge, angling above the valley. Maybe once we get around that shoulder, we'll see another, higher valley. Sound good to you?"

Clarisse shrugged again. "That's as good a plan as any. Truth is they could be anywhere. We're operating solely off luck here."

Clarisse was hoping to locate one of the shy and elusive packs of wolves that had naturalized to Yellowstone. Her passion for photography had eventually intertwined with her love of animals and she had gained some renown in photographic circles for her images of wild animals in their natural habitats. She desperately wanted to capture the wolves and add them to her impressive collection. There were already three magazines that had expressed an interest in purchasing the pictures and a related article if she should succeed.

Working together, Dale and Clarisse broke camp quickly. "Let's get a picture before we leave," Clarisse suggested, setting up the tripod and mounting her camera.

"All right," Dale agreed. "You get it set up. I think we should stand on that big boulder over there. Isn't it odd how it's the only one standing all alone in this valley?"

Clarisse eyed the boulder in question. It sat about twenty yards from the small stream, thrusting up from a large square shaped base in an almost anvil configuration, the broad flat top wider than the narrower base. Dale had climbed it the previous evening and that was how he had spied the trailhead on the far side of the valley.

"All right," she agreed and began searching for the best angle for the camera so the rising sun would be behind. While she set up the tripod, Dale clambered to the top of the anvil and gave her some playful poses while she got the focus and settings on the camera to her satisfaction.

Finally pleased that she had everything set correctly, Clarisse approached the boulder. The top flat section was easily five feet over her head, and she could see no way to scale up this side.

"You'll need to go around to the other side," Dale explained. "It's still pretty tall but I was able to find some handholds and pull myself up."

She trailed around and found where the far side of the boulder had a crack that gave just enough room to get her hiking boot into a toehold and a convenient handhold about a foot above her head that she was able to reach easily. Pulling herself up, she was grateful when Dale's extended hand grasped hers and pulled her the remainder of the way. "That's quite a climb!" she exclaimed breathlessly and then gasped at the splendor of the valley floor spread below them. Tiny tendrils of mist were rising from the surface of the cold stream where the morning sun was heating the air and the sun sparkled off a million drops of dew across the narrow vale. "It's so beautiful, Dale!"

"Yes, it certainly is."

She heard the warmth in his voice, and turning, found his eyes fixed on her. "Oh, you," she said softly, feeling warmth rise in her cheeks.

"What's this? A blush?" he asked, his fingers trailing across her cheek and brushing a stray tendril of hair back behind her ear. "And us married all of fifteen years!"

She smiled and stood on tiptoe to kiss him and pull him into a hug. "You can still make me blush," she murmured into his ear before stepping back and saying in a firmer voice, "Now come on and let's get this picture or we'll be here all day!"

"Yes, ma'am!"

A few minutes later Clarisse had taken several shots using the remote that triggered the shutter. "Now help me down and let's get a move on!"

Dale descended first, using the same spot to get down that they'd used to climb up. Going down was a lot harder than going up and Clarisse was a little afraid of heights. The first step down was the worst since Dale couldn't help her from where he was on the ground below. She laid on her stomach, legs hanging over the side, trying to find a toehold. "A little to your left," Dale called helpfully, and she finally located a solid ledge and began to slowly work her way down. When she was close enough, she felt Dale's hands grasp her around the waist and she let her weight fall back as he swung her clear. As her feet hit the ground, she turned to start across the valley, but found Dale bent over, hands supporting himself on his knees, a strained expression on his face.

"Dale? Are you okay?" she was instantly concerned, reaching out to grasp his shoulders.

He shook his head, "Fine. I'm fine. Just a muscle, I think." Slowly he straightened, holding his left arm a little close to his side as he did. He shot her a reassuring grin. "Not as young as I used to be, and we've been pretty physical the last twenty-four hours. Come on. We can get around that shoulder before lunch if we step lively."

Clarisse estimated that her step lost its liveliness somewhere around the quarter mile mark. The trail had at first started on a gradual incline that quickly became quite steep and in spots almost nearly vertical. At a half mile she felt fully winded and finally called out to Dale, "I need to stop. Need a drink of water."

He glanced back, his face beaded in sweat even though the morning was still quite cool, and nodded, "I could use a breather myself." He paused and scanned the trail ahead. "There's a nice flat rock about a hundred feet up. Should be a good spot to sit. Looks to have a good view."

Clarisse looked at the rock and groaned silently to herself. It seemed so far away. Hiding her disappointment from Dale, she smiled and nodded, "Looks good."

It really was a small distance to cover and in a short while Clarisse sat gratefully, drinking water still cold from having been immersed in the stream overnight, enjoying the view. The land below the boulder they sat on fell off sharply, and the nearest trees were much farther down the slope, while more tall pines bracketed them to the right and the left, providing a slim but clear view across the narrow valley they had just left. Clarisse noticed the anvil-shaped boulder jutting up next to the thin thread of stream. "I'll call it Anvil Valley," she announced softly.

"What's that?" Dale asked, eyes scanning the upper tree line of the ridge opposite.

"The valley we stayed in last night. I'm going to call it Anvil Valley. That boulder was shaped liked an anvil."

"I like it." He smiled and leaned over for a quick kiss. "And I *loved* last night."

Clarisse smiled and twined her fingers in his, lifting his hand to kiss the roughened knuckles. "I love you. Let me get a picture of Anvil Valley from here." Quickly she pulled her camera out of her pack and took several pictures, returning the camera before shouldering the backpack into place. "Okay. Ready if you are!"

They continued up the trail, winding through thick stands of massive firs, branches far above their heads blocking the warming sunlight, occasionally emerging along bare patches of rock snaking across the mountain shoulder. They had just emerged into one of these sunlit patches when Clarisse's stomach gave a large and aggravated growl. She giggled and Dale laughed outright.

"What's that you say?" he asked humorously.

"How embarrassing!" Clarisse exclaimed. "It's this mountain air. I've got twice my normal appetite."

Dale glanced at his watch. "It's too early for lunch. We are not eating lunch at ten in the morning. Think you can make it a bit longer?"

As if on cue, Clarisse's stomach grumbled again. "Oh goodness!" she giggled.

Dale laughed and answered the question himself. "I guess not." He looked around and shrugged. "This is a good spot to take a break. We've got some sunlight to warm us…which after being under those trees I could use a bit of warming. It's pretty cool. Feels good walking but a bit chilly."

"Yeah. My hands are a bit cold." Clarisse tucked them into her armpits.

They shrugged out of their backpacks and Clarisse stretched in relief. The pack was not especially heavy, but she was unaccustomed to it and the steep trail was difficult enough without also feeling out of balance. Her hiking boots felt like twenty-pound weights at the end of her legs. She slumped against a large rock and pulled two energy bars from the front pocket of her backpack, extending one to Dale in exchange for the bottle of water he held out. "Need to stay hydrated," he reminded her.

She nodded. So far, she had not been bothered with symptoms of altitude sickness, but it had happened to her before. Staying very hydrated was supposed to help. She drank deeply, tore open her energy bar and surveyed the view. The valley was no longer visible, having disappeared as they climbed higher. Now she could see the more distant mountain ridges, granite sides thrusting sharply into the clear sky to their west. The sun was shining on the granite and it gleamed a shade of pink in the mid-morning sun.

"I have to get a picture of that!" She set aside her energy bar and water, grabbing her camera and quickly snapping off a quick series at different settings. Then she put the camera away and just enjoyed the beauty as she finished the energy bar and water. "You've been quiet," she commented.

Dale smiled at her and replied, "Just enjoying this. It's such a beautiful place. Feels good to get a workout, too." His right hand absently massaged his left shoulder.

Clarisse nodded and laughed, "Yeah. I can definitely tell I need to do some toning. This is a good start, but when we get home, I'm going to have to make some changes."

Dale grinned, "I like where you're going."

She raised her eyebrows defensively and he held his hands up quickly, warding her off. "Not that I'm not happy just the way you are. But toned? Oh my!" He gave her a purely provocative eyebrow waggle and grinned. She couldn't help but join his laughter.

"Well? Are you ready, my love?" he finally asked, and she nodded, picking up her pack in response.

Dale grabbed his pack and began to sling it over his left shoulder when Clarisse suddenly saw him slump, body curling in over his stomach, left shoulder dropping towards the ground.

"Dale?" she cried, dropping her pack and lurching to her feet, quickly reaching his side and stooping in front of him. "Dale? Talk to me!"

Dale sat, his right hand clutching his left bicep, mouth gaping and Clarisse could hear his struggle to draw in air. His face was sheet white and his lips were tinged with blue. In alarm Clarisse urged him to sit on the trail and lie back. He resisted, not able to breathe on his back, fighting to turn on his side and curl over on his left, quickly tossing to the right when the pressure was too intense on his laboring heart.

Clarisse was paralyzed, uncertain what to do. It was obvious Dale was having a heart attack. She only knew the very basics of first aid and didn't know what to do. She held his head in her lap, keeping it off the sharp stones in the path, trying to cradle him. She kept repeating, "Relax, Dale. Try to breath calmly. Try, honey. Come on. Come on. Relax."

Instead, she felt him stiffen. She heard him exhale and she waited tensely for him to inhale. And waited. And waited. She realized tears where streaming down her face, her own heart suddenly ached horribly in her chest, but it was no heart attack. It was the first murmur of grief.

"Dale? No, Dale. No, no, no, Dale!" She dropped his head to the ground and gently rolled him on his back, seeing his eyes open, stare fixed far over her head. "Dale, you listen to me!" She was angry now, "Don't you do this!" She lowered her head to his mouth, cheek close to the parted lips, hoping to feel any wisp. Her fingers groped at his wrist for a pulse but could not find any.

She tried to administer mouth to mouth. She tilted his head back as she remembered they had told them when she took the First Aid class offered free at work one day. She even tried to do the chest compressions. She feared she didn't have the requisite strength. She recalled that they had told them in class that day that it takes enough force to break the sternum cage to properly get the strength needed to compress the heart. All your doing is hitting a cage of bone otherwise.

After a while Clarisse finally gave up. Her body was exhausted, she had spots in her vision, and she was struggling with catching her own breath. Weakly she struggled back to her feet and stumbled to the nearest boulder that she could lean against, weight sagging against the hard surface. Slowly her body recovered. Her breathing returned to normal, her vision cleared. She took a deep breath, mind still reeling. Dale dead! Her mind did not want to accept this harsh reality. At any moment she expected to hear him say, "Come on, darling. Let's pick up the pace!" Silence reigned in the bright morning sunlight.

Clarisse glanced back at Dale, body awkwardly twisted half on his right side, half on his back, in the middle of the trail where she had left him. She was thankful she could not see his eyes from where she sat. Her heart pulled in her chest and a sob burst from her. She remembered how he had teased her when they'd watched some documentary on television that stated green eyes were so rare only two percent of the population had them. He'd told her how lucky she was to be loved by a two percenter. She would never again see those green eyes look at her filled with love, or mischief, or the occasional brief flare of irritation that happens when two people live together. Yes, she would miss even the worst of him as she had loved the best of him. He had been such a good man. And yes, she had been lucky.

Another spasm of pain seized her; she could feel her heart pulling in her chest. A sob burst out and she bent over, hugging herself tight as her body shook with fierce sobs. Eventually she slumped to her knees and curled over, rocking gently until the pain passed. She stayed huddled for a while.

Again, her body stilled, and her mind slowly calmed. A cold and logical part of her brain, the part concerned with survival, took control. She had to get a grip. She was in a precarious situation and she needed to get her wits about her.

Carefully she sat up, sitting back on her heels, and surveyed her surroundings with a new eye. She didn't wear a watch and she didn't want to think about trying to look at Dale's, she wasn't ready for that yet. She glanced at the sun but knew, even as she did so, that it was pointless. She had no idea what was north and couldn't begin to guess the time just from the position of the sun. Then it occurred to her. Her camera. Pulling it from her backpack she quickly thumbed it on and went to the settings screen. The information window displayed the time as ten forty-five. Automatically Clarisse calculated that it had been close to ten when they'd stopped. A new habit in life was formed. How much time had elapsed?

Self-survival took control before Clarisse could spiral into another episode of grief. She grimly checked the settings on her camera and focused on Dale's inert form, forcing herself to remain calm and take the picture. It would help to establish his time of death.

Wearily she pushed away from the boulder and walked back to him, circling so she stood at his feet, and took another series of quick shots. Returning to her backpack she carefully returned the camera to its padded case. Almost immediately she wondered what time it was. She thrust the thought aside angrily, recognizing that her mind was fixating on time in order to escape dealing with the present.

Grimly she surveyed the location. The rocky grade formed a bare oval shape on the steep slope of the mountain, trees encroaching on all sides with a total cleared space of what looked like less than an acre. A few dead trees, darkened husks protruding over the rocks and boulders, had a burnt look as if they may have been victims of a forest fire in the distant past. While Clarisse spied a lot of good dead wood at hand, her mind instantly rejected the location as unsuitable. The forest edge was too close to risk a large fire.

Her eyes wandered back to Dale. Quickly she did the math in her head. Thirty hours would be around four in the afternoon tomorrow. At best she would have until ten tomorrow night. They had spent the entire previous day hiking in from the Ranger Station where they had parked their Explorer and they had been making good time, covering a lot of ground. That first section of the hike had been mostly level ground and the valley they had camped in had been at a slight elevation. She seemed to recall the last hour or so of the hike had begun to wind uphill and she was glad when they'd reached the relatively level floor of the little valley. She figured they had progressed about another mile up the shoulder of the mountain this morning.

Could she make it back to the Ranger Station today? And, even if she did, was there any hope of getting back here with help by four in the afternoon tomorrow? She realized in despair that it simply wasn't possible. She was going to have to deal with this without any assistance. Even if she got to the Ranger Station today there was no guarantee anyone would even be there. It was an unmanned station and she'd have to use the emergency phone to signal help.

Clarisse tried to remember everything she could about the phenomenon of reanimation. It had all started on December thirteenth in 2012. At early dawn on December thirteenth, in Queensland Australia, a woman spotted figures moving about in the Nudgee Catholic Cemetery. There was something a bit odd about them.

The sun had not fully risen and in the weak light the woman was only able to make out that some of the figures appeared to be drunken, shambling aimlessly between the head stones. The dirt of the only major private cemetery in Brisbane was torn up in a haphazard manner and the woman thought at first that the people she was seeing must be grave robbers that had gotten intoxicated while pursuing their nefarious activities. She drove to the Queensland Police station at Fortitude Valley to report the suspicious activity and then went on about her business.

The Queensland police dispatched a unit to the cemetery and in short order backup was requested due to the size of the crowd now milling about in the cemetery. One of the policemen got a bit too close and the crowd seized him. As his fellow officer's watched, he was torn limb from limb, as the crowd began cannibalizing him. The police began shooting into the crowd and couldn't understand why their bullets were having no effect, until one of them shot a scraggly looking fellow in the head, dropping his target to the ground, where it remained. The body lying there in the rising sun was little more than a skeleton. There could be no doubt of what the stunned policemen were looking at, the autopsy stitching clearly visible on many of the shambling corpses in the early morning light. Only then did they begin to understand the horror of what they were seeing. While the officers were fighting this battle more reports began coming in as the sun relentlessly marched across Australia...heralding in a new dawn for the age of humanity.

Fortunately for most Americans news spread faster than the sun travels, so they were not completely taken by surprise when December thirteenth dawned for them and graveyards around the country began regurgitating their dead. Of course, there were casualties, and it took many months for the world to adjust. It never did return to the way it was. The dead would not remain dead and it took some trial and error before people managed to restore order to their world.

No one could be sure what had caused the dead to rise...and continue to rise. Many rumors had begun in early 2012. The Mayan calendar ended on December twelfth and there were many people that believed the world would end on that date.

The religious pundits claimed we were at the beginning of the seven years of Tribulations. We had witnessed the greatest event and the most incredible of all of God's miracles. We had witnessed The Rapture. The risen bodies were evidence of their soul's being called home to God. The reanimated, gruesome shells the detritus left behind, seeking out the worthiest to send their souls to God as well. In our disbelief we were repudiating the very thing that could have delivered us from the days of darkness to come. By our own hand's we had sent God's most righteous to live at His side in glory. They quoted a hopeful message though:

"But let me tell you a wonderful secret God has revealed to us. Not all of us will die, but we will all be transformed. It will happen in a moment, in the blinkful of an eye.
1 Corinthians 15:51-52 – Holy Bible (NLT)

Other's thought it had to be a government plot; some strain of virus released. Yet, on that day, the dead rose as the sun made its circle around the earth and no country was left spared.

The reanimated corpses were not especially fast, nor were they very coordinated. A living person who remained aware of his surroundings could easily elude them. They were not strong and could not batter down locked doors. They found climbing stairs extremely difficult, though if they were determined enough, they could manage it. The fresher a corpse, the nimbler it seemed to be. As a rule, they all shared one overwhelming hunger...the taste of living, human flesh. The ones that were truly dangerous were the ones that had most recently died. The dead that had yet to be interred and were awaiting burial in morgues were the ones most successful at adding a few victims to their ranks. The monstrosities they created from their feasting were gruesome with large chunks of flesh torn away. The zombies could not readily reach the brain through the hard shell of the skull and so while their victims died from the cannibalistic attack, they did not remain dead.

Scientists quickly identified the timelines for reanimation, and it was rapidly communicated throughout the communities of the world. If you wished to keep someone dead, you had roughly thirty to thirty-six hours to ensure they stayed dead. You either cremated the bodies or decapitated them. Those with a lot of money could of course choose the much more expensive solution of having the brain removed and destroyed.

As predicted by the Bible, we did not all die. People are survivors and approximately half the world's population survived. More in highly developed countries while far fewer in the world's third world countries. In those areas, the losses were shockingly high with entire communities vanishing.

Clarisse shook herself from her reveries and glanced at the sky. She couldn't make it to the Ranger Station, and she couldn't risk a fire in this small open patch. She would need to move Dale to a better spot. She couldn't remember anything suitable once they'd left the valley floor and she decided wearily she would have to retrace their path back to Anvil Valley. Quickly she foraged for three suitable limbs in the nearby forest and used the length of twine they always tucked into their backpacks to fashion a travois.

She laid the travois on the rough ground next to Dale's twisted form, knotted the corners of the spread they used for their picnic lunches and dinners so it would hold Dale's body, and struggled to roll him onto the lumpy frame she'd built. Finally, she had him centered between the two long poles she would hold, and she pulled her backpack over her tired shoulders, ignoring the throbbing ache of her abused muscles. She levered Dale's backpack onto the travois, and grimly grasped the rough limbs in each hand, using her legs to help as she strained to lift the travois into position. She staggered a bit at the weight, and heard an ominous creak from the wood, but the frame held, as did she. Carefully she took her first step.

It wasn't long before Clarisse's hands were burning from the rough bark of the limbs. As the sun climbed high overhead the air beneath the high boughs of the massive fir trees became humid and she wished for a breeze. She wanted to reach the spot where she had taken that last picture of Anvil Valley before she allowed herself a break.

It seemed to take hours to reach the spot. Carefully Clarisse lowered the travois onto the decayed log of a tree that was green with moss, leaving Dale at an inclined angle in the shade of the trees. She ventured alone to the jutting boulder, dismayed at how far away the green valley appeared from this height. She drank deeply from the now tepid bottle of water, remembering how refreshing it had been just a few short hours ago. She glanced at the distant mountain peak to the west and noted the sun was quite a bit closer. She turned and strode resolutely to the travois, reaching for the watch on Dale's left arm, trying to swallow the sudden lump in her throat.

Clarisse shuddered and grasped his arm, shocked again by how the feel of him was so terribly different. She had never touched a corpse before, and the experience was dreadfully disturbing. Her fingers fumbled on the strap, struggling to pop the small bar from the worn leather. Dale's arm felt wooden beneath her fingers, the flesh resisting her pressure unnaturally. She felt slightly nauseated and almost staggered back before lowering her head and focusing again on the cracked leather. She had been meaning to get him a new watch this coming Christmas. Quickly she snuffed the thought and turned back to the sunny boulder. It was a quarter past two and she had covered a little more than half the distance.

She leaned against the boulder, resting. As she stood there, a slight breeze rose, it's gentle stir cooling her face. She closed her eyes and lifted her face gratefully. Running her hands through her hair, pushing it back from her sweaty forehead. She cried out as she felt the burn as her hair brushed the tender skin of her palms. Inspecting her hands, she found them raw and red, tiny particles of rotten wood lodged painfully in open scrapes. She retrieved a clean cotton tee shirt from her backpack and a fresh bottle of water. She cleaned her hands as well as she could and then tore the tee shirt into long strips, pouring water over the strips of cloth before wrapping the wet material around her tender hands.

She looked out over the distant valley and then surveyed the path winding down over the shoulder she sat on. It was very steep here and the travois would be awkward to maneuver. By her guesstimate it had taken the best part of two hours to cover the distance and she had a good half mile left to cover. Allowing for the difficulty of the terrain she thought she'd be doing well to reach the valley before dusk. This early in the spring, dusk settled quickly with the tall mountain ridge blocking the western horizon.

Clarisse was not hungry, but she felt tremors in her muscles and knew she needed to eat something. She dug a granola bar out of her pack and washed it down with the last of the water, tucking both empties into the small bag hanging from her pack that she used for any garbage on the trail and walked back to resume her burden.

Her hands hurt tremendously, and she moaned aloud at the pain as the weight of the travois settled fully into her aching palms. Even with the cloth protecting them she could feel the rough bark pressing painfully into the now open flesh. Gritting her teeth and biting back another cry of pain Clarisse forced herself to move forward.

Dale was not a very large man, but at five feet eleven inches, and boasting a well-toned muscular frame, he outweighed her by nearly seventy pounds. The travois had been difficult enough to pull along the rudimentary trail. The branches kept catching on every root and stone, jerking roughly against her hands, the full weight bearing heavily on her shoulders. Even though she was moving downhill her progress had been distressingly slow.

Finally, Clarisse could see the trees thinning and the ground did seem to be leveling out. She lowered Dale and stretched her back, back arming sweat off her forehead. Glancing at the watch, she saw it was four twenty-three. The sun was now touching the trees on that far ridge and she figured she had about two hours to decide how she was going to secure Dale's body for the night.

Leaving his body on the trail she walked the rest of the way down the slope and stopped at the edge of the small valley. They must have gotten here at about the same time last night. The quality of light was very similar to what she recalled from the previous evening when they first stepped into the valley from the southern end, roughly opposite to where she was standing now.

Three deer stood next to the stream, unaware of her presence. Two drank while a third kept watchful eyes on the tree line to the west, alert for any movement. Clarisse shifted her weight forward slightly, automatically reaching for the camera normally on her shoulder, her photographic instincts naturally taking over. The camera was still in the backpack and she shook her head wearily. This was no time to think about taking pictures of deer.

No longer concerned at maintaining silence, she stepped out into the valley. The deer froze, gazing across the glen at her, and then, as silent as snowflakes, they took flight back into the woods.

Clarisse surveyed the valley, looking for a likely spot to secure Dale's body for the night. Ideally, it needed to be high enough to be out of reach of bears or buried deep enough that bears or wolves couldn't dig it up. She was not strong enough for either task, she feared.

Close to where they had pitched their tent was the large anvil shaped boulder and Clarisse hoped she might find some way of using it. She crossed to it and shrugged off her backpack. The boulder was almost twice her height and not easy to climb, yet they had scaled it this morning. She circled the base, looking for the spot where Dale had made his ascent. Finally, she located the crack, and began hauling herself up.

Once at the summit she surveyed the valley, fighting tears at first, and then finally succumbing to the grief overwhelming her. She sobbed, her body trembling with the force of her sorrow, until she was weak and drained. Her vision narrowed and spots danced. She knew she was close to passing out, hyperventilating as she gasped for air, reduced now to the choking sobs of a child in a tantrum. She curled over her knees, folding into a small ball on top of the boulder, while she slowly regained control of herself. This was no time for hysterics.

Gradually she calmed though her head still felt as though it were swathed in cotton and her vision had shadows at the edges like a picture with a vignette filter. She surveyed the top of the boulder and then scanned the valley, seeking a place where she might be able to secure Dale until tomorrow, when she would build his funeral pyre. There were several trees with limbs low enough that she thought she might be able to hang his body out of reach of any predators. She had rope enough but she wasn't sure she had strength enough for the task. Of course, hauling him to the top of the boulder would be even harder.

Scrambling down, Clarisse returned to where she'd left Dale on the trail and once again bent to the task of dragging him the remainder of the way. From there she chose a tree whose limbs were high enough and yet also sturdy enough to hold his weight. It took three tries to finally throw a length of rope over the high limb and once she had both ends securely in hand, she tested its strength with her own weight. The limb groaned in protest but held. With trembling hands Clarisse formed a slip knot in one end and secured it around Dale's chest, under his arms. Then, taking the other end in her hand she began trying to pull Dale's body off the ground. It was harder than she had imagined, the rope not wanting to slide over the rough bark of the branch and her body weight was much less than Dale's.

Slowly, Dale's body began to lift. The strain on Clarisse was tremendous, but she knew she could not relent, could not rest...to lose even an inch would cost more energy than she had in reserve. Pulling the rope over her shoulder, she turned and threw all her weight against the rope, forcing herself to step forward and she began to gain ground. The weight on the rope became even greater and she felt the rope burning into her shoulder. Looking back, she saw that Dale was now almost upright. If she could just gain another five feet it would be enough.

Turning back, leaning into the rope, she rested for a moment before heaving with all her strength. She gained some momentum. Perversely, once Dale was off the ground, pulling him seemed to be easier. Perhaps there was less resistance. In any event, it was working and after another twenty minutes of effort Dale's feet were about three and a half feet off the ground. Not wanting to risk his dropping, Clarisse immediately circled the tree, pulling the rope taut around the trunk. Once she had circled the base twice, she awkwardly began knotting the rope as tightly as possible. Finally, the job was done, and Dale's body hung swaying from the tree limb. He was by no means out of reach of a bear, but it would be difficult for smaller predators to reach him. Wolves would no doubt be able to reach his legs, but she didn't think they'd be able to pull him down. It would have to do.

She turned and went back to the brook. Kneeling beside the rushing water she doused her face and arms in the icy stream, the sudden cold shocking her and momentarily stealing her breath. The ice water felt good on her burned and throbbing hands. She sat back on her heels and again surveyed the valley.

Darkness was quickly encroaching. Deep shadows now lay under the trees and Clarisse thought she saw furtive movement wherever she looked. She knew it was only her imagination but as night began to descend, she became more aware of how dangerous her situation was. A woman alone, in the middle of the forest, with a dead body that would begin attracting some very unwelcome company.

She returned to her backpack and checked the camera. She would have to preserve evidence for the authorities later. Turning the camera on, she accessed the pictures she had taken. The camera's metadata marked Dale's time of death and she would need that to explain her actions. Turning the camera off, she opened the small door securing the memory card and slipped it out. She pulled a small metal box the size of a wallet out of her backpack and opening it, slipped the memory card into the slot expressly for that purpose. Then she put the metal wallet into an inner pocket of the backpack. She couldn't risk losing it.

She ate two more energy bars and opened another bottle of water. It was getting too late and too dark to think about setting up the tent, but she needed to get a small fire going. That should be enough to keep any animals away. Mechanically she gathered wood and set about making a small fire next to the stream. Once the flames were licking hungrily at the dry tinder, she added some bigger limbs she dragged from the underbrush and then she spread the sleeping bag out on the ground next to the fire. She didn't really think she would sleep but she knew she needed to rest.

Exhaustion took over and Clarisse slipped into a deep and dreamless sleep. The sun woke her the next morning and she woke with a start. A feeling almost of guilt stole over her at the thought that she could have slept at all while her dead husband's body dangled like a gruesome ornament from the tree where she had left him.

The sleep had done her good and she felt much better for having rested. She was weak from exhaustion and hunger all the same. She had only consumed those four energy bars yesterday, plus the bowl of oatmeal for breakfast, and this morning her body was demanding that she feed it. She knew she needed to eat if she hoped to have the energy to accomplish what needed to be done. Her small fire from the previous night had burned out and not even hot coals remained.

Gathering more tinder, Clarisse got the fire going again and hauled out enough branches to get a decent flame going. She consumed a quick breakfast of oatmeal while a small pot of coffee brewed. As she ate, she mulled over her options.

She figured she was down to about twelve hours before Dale would reanimate. Not nearly enough time to get him back to the Rangers Station. Even if she could, there might not be anyone there. No, she still had only one choice left to her. Clarisse felt around inside the backpack, confirming the metal wallet was still securely zippered inside the inner pocket.

A year after the first reanimations a woman had been arrested in northwest Arkansas for suspected murder. She claimed her husband had died unexpectedly and she had no means of getting help. They had lived in a remote cabin deep in the Ozarks with no phone. Her husband had been a large man and she had struggled unsuccessfully with dragging his body out of the cabin. Their only vehicle was an old, manual transmission truck and she did not know how to drive it. Not knowing what else to do she had taken an ax and chopped off his head. She had then hiked several miles to the main road and a gas station where someone had finally called the police.

There had been no evidence supporting her claim and the poor woman had faced a trial. There was a terrible media blitz. In the end, she was found not guilty, but the media campaign had been so fierce, and the national coverage so intense, that she was unable to live with the stigmatism of society and ended up committing suicide.

The result had been new laws. Couples quickly signed what was called a Living Dead Will expressing their desire that their spouse or significant other should dispose of them if necessary, in the event of sudden death, to ensure they did not reanimate. This would protect the surviving partner but even so, that was not enough. There needed to be clear evidence that the surviving partner had no other choice.

Clearly, Clarisse was in just such a situation herself right now and she would need to prove her innocence once she returned to civilization. Fortunately, both she and Dale had been practical and there were Living Wills, Living Dead Wills and Final Wills all on file with their attorney.

Pulling herself from her thoughts, she began the task of gathering enough wood. First, she scavenged all the wood she could haul from the surrounding area, moving farther up into the mountain to gather more. It was early afternoon by the time she had gathered what she deemed to be enough.

Starting with a layer of larger limbs, she made a square of wood roughly seven feet by three feet and then she cut the rope suspending Dale. His body was in full rigor and for a dreadful moment he was balanced on his feet, his dead body standing for what seemed like forever before he toppled forward onto his face. His body struck the ground with terrible force, bouncing at impact, and Clarisse gave a cry of grief. Once again sobs threatened to overwhelm her.

Bringing herself under control, not allowing herself to think of what she was doing, she turned him over, gripped him again around the chest and hauled him over to the wood she had laid out, stumbling over the large limbs and dislodging most of them in the process. Dropping his body, she forced limbs under him and around him and then hauled the remainder of the wood over him...forming a large pyre in the middle of the valley, away from the encroaching trees.

She was surprised how late in the day it was. It was already close to three in the afternoon and it had already been almost thirty hours. She was running out of time. The hard work was done now. All that remained was to light the fire and watch him burn.

Clarisse retrieved her camera and the memory card, slipped the card back in, and fighting a sudden surge of nausea took more pictures; pictures of the pyre, Dale's body clearly visible under his shroud of wood. Then she returned the card to its wallet and the camera to the backpack, sitting down beside the pyre.

She had thought this would be the easy part. She realized now that all that had gone before had been the easy part. This was the truly hard part and she wasn't sure she could carry it through.

She picked up the small tin can of lighter fluid, and then set the can on the ground beside her. Hugging her knees to her chest, Clarisse again allowed herself to grieve. She knew this was what Dale would have wanted her to do. He would never want to come back as a shambling, mindless, animated corpse.

She realized the first thing he would do would be to come after her. She tried to envision what that would be like. Tried to imagine him bearing down on her. His teeth gnashing at her throat until he succeeded in killing her. As hard as she tried, she could not imagine it.

They had shared a special bond. She knew Dale to be kind hearted. A man who tended to be quiet spoken and slow to anger. She could not imagine him now as a bloodthirsty, mindless creature. How could she possibly light this pile of wood, burning the man she loved to cinders?

As the sun dropped lower in the sky, something gleamed in the pile of wood. It caught her eye and she recognized Dale's wedding band. It struck her that she could not bear to have nothing left of him, that she wanted his wedding ring, to have something more than memories and old photos.

She clawed her way through the wood until she reached his hand. The ring was tight and didn't want to slide over his knuckle. Shuddering a little over her own actions, Clarisse spit into her own palm and then carefully greased the ring and twisted it back and forth; pulling until it finally came off in her hand. Clumsily, not feeling her own tears, she shoved the ring into the front pocket of her jeans and then resumed her seat. The sun had almost set now and still she could not bring herself to light the wood on fire.

Dropping her head onto her knees, hugging them to her chest, she tried to hold in her grief and pain. Suddenly from the west ridge she heard a loud crashing sound. Jerking upright she scanned the tree line trying not to panic. The sound of wood breaking continued and was all too obviously moving in her direction. Quickly she reached for Dale's backpack, the gun still lying somewhere inside, hoping she wouldn't need it, praying it would be enough.

Her trembling fingers felt the cold metal of the barrel and she carefully pulled the weapon out of the pack, her eyes never leaving the tree line, now able to see where small saplings were moving as something forced its way towards her.

She checked the gun; a forty-five revolver Dale had picked up shortly after they met, and they had started taking road trips. He had taught her how to use it even though she had been a reluctant learner. He would always preach to her how important it might be one day in saving their lives. So, she had learned. She saw now that the gun was loaded. She released the safety and kept the gun pointed safely to one side as Dale had taught her.

An enormous brown bear emerged across the clearing from her. Her mind frantically went through her short catalogue of knowledge on bears.

What had she always heard other than using pepper spray? Don't run. Make yourself seem large and menacing. Make a lot of noise.

Her throat was suddenly dry and constricted and she doubted she'd be able to do more than squeak if she tried. But guns make noise...and lots of it. She knew better than to try and shoot the bear. At best, she'd probably only injure it and make it angry. An angry injured bear was not something she wished to try to deal with.

Instead, she began waving her arms, managed to find her voice after all and shouted at it. Then she discharged the gun safely into the air. The bear was startled, lowered its head to the ground, shaking its shaggy coat and seemed at first undecided on what to do. Then it shambled to the stream and slapped its front feet down, raising a spray of water and faced her again.

She continued yelling senselessly, no real words, just loud shouts verging on screams, and discharged the gun again. This time the bear seemed to decide she might be more trouble than she was worth, and turning its back, shuffled off across the clearing into the woods on the edge of the eastern ridge. Clarisse listened hard until she could no longer hear anything and determined the bear had gone away. Hopefully it wouldn't decide to come back.

She was abruptly consumed with uncontrollable shudders. Knowing it was delayed shock, her body reacting to the threat from the bear, overwhelmed with released adrenalin, she sank back to the ground until the shudders subsided.

The sun was now almost fully set. She could delay no longer; Dale could possibly reanimate at any time. Glancing at the watch, she saw it was shortly before seven. Almost thirty-three hours had passed, and she knew she was out of time.

Once she set the pyre burning, she wouldn't need to worry about animals. Neither bears nor wolves would approach a blaze this size. Without allowing herself time to think she doused the wood with lighter fluid. Circling the pyre, squirting the fluid over the wood, until the can was empty. And still she couldn't find the courage to light it.

Then, from somewhere off in the dark woods she heard a long, shrill howl and from a position slightly to the side of the first one, another haunting howl lifted into the night sky. The wolves were making their presence known and Clarisse did not trust her own abilities to believe she could shoot a running wolf in the dark. She had to act, and she had to do it now.

As she arrived at her decision, she heard the snap of a twig at her back. Swinging around, she saw with horror that she had delayed too long. Dale's arm, visible where she had pulled the wood aside to reach his hand, had moved and as she watched it moved again.

"Oh, God! Dale, no. No, no, no!" Feeling hysteria rise within her, knowing she was left with no options, she quickly fumbled for the large torch

67

lighter they used to light their campfires. At first her fingers wouldn't obey. They couldn't manipulate the child safety mechanism and also pull the trigger to release the flame.

Meanwhile, Dale was beginning to move more, and Clarisse knew she had only moments and then the decision would no longer be in her control. She finally managed to hold the child safety catch and pull the trigger. Flame burst from the end of the lighter, igniting one of the branches. Clarisse stepped back a safe distance. She watched with horror as the small flame she had ignited on the branch began to die out. The branch had not had enough tinder around it to sustain the tiny flame.

Dale's flailing arm was now clearly visible, and he began to lever himself out from under the wood. It would not be a difficult task. She hadn't thought to haul in any heavy stumps to weight the body down. She hadn't thought it would be necessary when she was dragging in the limbs she found scattered on the ground. She seemed to have a wealth of time at that moment.

She paused, uncertain what her next action should be. The tiny flame once again leapt up out of the branch and another twig nearby caught the infant spark. It may still catch...but not nearly soon enough. Clarisse needed an alternate course of action immediately. Dale had almost extricated himself from the stack of wood and his green eyes had already sought her out. She had circled around, and the stack was between them. He began to scramble back into the pile in the most direct attempt to reach her.

Satisfied the pile of wood would slow him down; she took a quick moment to assess her situation. Dale and the stack of wood were between her and the gun. Behind her and about forty feet away was the boulder. She grabbed one of the backpacks as she ran past them, shrugging it over her good shoulder and hoping it was the one with water and food. There was no telling how long she might be stranded on the boulder. Clarisse quickly found the handhold and clawed her way to the top, scanning the scene below her.

The pyre suddenly flared up as the tiny flame caught the fumes of lighter fluid in an area she had soaked down. Between the fire and boulder came the lurching shape of a man. A man she had loved for almost two decades. A man that now craved nothing more in this world than to have her join him in his eternal hunger. Clarisse knew there was little danger in his being able to scale the boulder. All the same, she'd better check to see if she had anything to stop him if he did try.

She dropped to her knees and opened the backpack. She saw with relief that she had grabbed the right one. Her camera was nestled on top of the emergency poncho and thermal blanket. Under the blanket she knew were several bottles of water and the remaining energy bars. Velcro straps held her tripod in place along the side and Clarisse fumbled it out of its case. It might be useful.

Meanwhile, Dale had stumbled to the foot of the boulder and was vainly reaching up the surface of the rock, trying to reach her. His green eyes seemed to implore her to join him. She searched but could find no evidence of intelligence in that gaze. His face was slack and vacant. A horrible mewling sound escaped from his gaping jaws. His fingers began clawing at the rock as she sat watching, transfixed with horror. The skin began to flay off the tips of his fingers as he relentlessly tried to reach her at the summit.

Sickened at the sight, she moved back from the edge to where she could no longer see him. His mewling cries became more frantic when he could no longer see her and she heard him begin moving around the base of the rock, seeking a point from which he might get to her. It took him a considerable amount of time to work his way fully around the circumference and she relaxed a little knowing he could not scale it. She sat in a huddle at the center, watching the fire.

As night descended, the air began to chill, and she longed for the warmth of the blaze. She was too far away for any of the heat to reach her on her rocky perch. She pulled the thermal blanket out and tugged it around her shoulders. Gradually the flames began to gutter and die down, until only embers glowed in the deepening night. Dale relentlessly continued his efforts to mount the boulder and as the crackling of the fire died away Clarisse could hear the sharp click as the bones in his fingers scraped the surface of the rock. As the smoke lifted from the narrow valley another scent began to intrude on Clarisse's senses and she knew it was the sickening odor of Dale's decaying body.

It was fully dark when, from the eastern ridge, Clarisse heard the distinctive sounds of a large animal moving. She knew she had not been the only one able to detect that scent. The bear had returned. She strained vainly in the darkness trying to see the far edge of the forest. The shadows were too deep and the fire a mere glow. Would the bear dare to come this close? A silence settled once more over the valley and only the gruesome sound of Dale's finger bones clawing at the rock and the faint sounds of his continued mewling reached her ears. Had the bear decided then to retreat or was it merely waiting for an opportune moment?

Time lost meaning for Clarisse. Minutes became hours as the night deepened around her and finally only embers remained, glowing feebly in the deep of night. She had begun to doze, her head dropping to her knees, no longer aware of the deep ache across her shoulders, or the fact that her legs were fast asleep from sitting in her hunched position for so long.

A fierce growl seemed to fill the night sounding as though it came from almost beneath her. She came fully awake with a start, her head rearing up, and her shoulders screaming silently in agony. A groan escaped her. The bear had advanced silently into the valley, drawn by the scent of freshly decaying meat. At the sound of her groan Dale redoubled his efforts to reach her, apparently ignorant of the threat at his back. She could see the massive bulk of the bear, darker against the darkness of the night. The moon cast enough light, though, for her to see more than she wanted to.

The bear was less than ten feet behind Dale; its massive jaws were open in a snarl, the huge canines reflecting the glint of the moon. As she watched, those jaws stretched and a massive, deep bellow came from the open maw of the beast. A strand of saliva depended from the jaw, dangling like a silver thread in the moonlight. Dale continued his senseless scrabbling, his dead brain not able to register the presence of the beast.

Clarisse watched in horror as the bear suddenly charged, its massive body slamming into Dale from behind. She felt the thud as the boulder absorbed the shock. Mercifully she could not see what damage the bear was inflicting. Dale's murmurs grew louder but there was no change in cadence, the mindless sounds only rising in volume. A part of her wished to save him, spare him the brutality of the attack, but to think such a thing was sheer madness. She knew that as horrible as the attack was, the bear was saving her life. This was her chance and it may be the only chance she would get.

Dale and the bear were on the side of the boulder towards the dying fire. Her egress from the boulder was on the opposite side and she could descend while Dale was occupied with the bear. If she could skirt the boulder and creep around to the other side of the fire, she could get the gun. Moving slowly, biting her teeth against the agony as circulation moved through her numbed legs, Clarisse made for the back of the boulder. From her position she stopped and listened intently. The only sounds were of Dale's mindless mumbling and the wet sound of the bear's rending jaws and occasional growls. The sounds of the struggle continued from the same location, roughly opposite to where she was perched. It did not sound as though Dale was aware of her movement and the bear was entirely absorbed.

Clarisse slipped down from the top of the boulder and upon reaching the ground pressed her back to the rock, holding her breath and listening intently for any sounds that would indicate either Dale or the bear was aware of her descent. Then, bending over so that she would be low to the ground, she sprinted towards the stream, not allowing herself to pause until she had reached its banks. There she dropped to the ground and turned her attention back to the boulder. From where she was lying, she could see the hind end of the bear.

Her movements had not attracted its attention. She could not see Dale from where she was and for that she was grateful. She turned next to see how best to approach the barely glowing embers of the fire. The gun should be lying on the ground roughly opposite to the boulder. There were some small scrub brushes growing on the banks of the stream and she could use those for cover. Hopefully she would be able to find the gun in the darkness.

She cautiously stepped across the small stream and gained the safety of the brush. Her trek around to the far side of the spot where the fire had burned, where Dale should have been safely cremated, seemed to take hours. As she advanced, she listened intently for any changes from the bear or from Dale. The wet tearing sounds seemed to go on forever and at some point, Dale's ceaseless murmuring died out. A silence descended on the valley, seeming to amplify every little sound Clarisse made as she navigated her way to the opposite side of the site of the bonfire.

As she approached there were only a few visible embers and the moon was waning, casting only a feeble light into the depression between the mountain ridges. It was enough light, however, to cast a gleam on the metal of the gun's barrel. Clarisse picked it up, amazed at how secure it suddenly made her feel. She strained to see the area at the base of the boulder, but it was too dark for her eyes to penetrate. She could only barely make out the large bulk of the bear. Keeping low, she retreated back across the stream and headed for the tree line, deciding to wait out the night under the cover of the trees.

Clarisse dozed and was awakened by the first rays of the sun as dawn crept over the eastern flank of the mountains. Birds were filling the morning light with song and for a moment she could not remember where she was or why she was sleeping sitting against the base of a towering pine tree, its coarse bark poking painfully into her spine.

The memories from the previous day were not long in returning and the beautiful dawn seemed to contradict those dark events. Grimly, she picked the revolver up from where it lay between her splayed legs. She could hear nothing from the valley floor behind her. Slowly she gained her feet and turned to face whatever lay in wait.

As she descended back into the valley, breaking from the line of trees into the clearing, she quickly surmised that the bear had departed at some point unbeknownst to her. Probably after she had dozed off. She could remember only too vividly the raw wet sounds and the occasional growls. She couldn't be absolutely certain, but she thought at one point the wolves must have made an appearance because she had heard the bear's rumblings evolve into fierce growls and grunts. There had seemed to be more than one creature growling and she knew at the time she wanted to believe it was wolves she heard and not her husband.

Approaching the wisps of smoke still rising from the spent bonfire, Clarisse was forced to look at the horrible, red mess at the base of the boulder. Surely whatever creature her husband had returned as, it could not have survived the brutality of what she was seeing. The torso was practically separated at the waist. The wet, red entrails of the intestines strewn across the ground in a wide radius. The thigh of one leg had been torn away and bone gleamed in the morning light above the remnants of the knee. One arm was missing entirely and only about a fourth of a stump remained of the other arm...the long shank of the forearm lying about three feet away.

Clarisse gagged and stumbled back to the creek. Falling to her knees, she vomited into the dewed grass at the verge of the stream. The heaves continued long after her exhausted body had anything to purge. Weakly she splashed the cold mountain water onto her face, briefly reveling in the refreshingly ice-cold water. She rinsed, spitting out the vile taste of her vomit. Weakly, she regained her feet, the gun still clutched in her hand.

Turning once more to the tattered remains of her husband, her stomach clenching yet again, she forced down her nausea, her legs trembling so badly she doubted her ability to cross the ground. She knew she should take a picture to document for the authorities, but she could not bear to do it. Bad enough she would have to ensure Dale was dead.

She was not long in discovering the awful truth. Overwhelmed by revulsion, Clarisse's eyes met Dale's green eyes, and she saw those eyes tracking her progress as she staggered back to the mangled corpse. Choking back dry heaves, she could not help but notice the stubs of the arms twitching towards her, even now the grotesque hunger consuming him. She resolutely raised the revolver, sighting in at the center of his forehead. She was less than forty feet from him and could not possibly miss at this range. Still, she wanted to be absolutely certain the bullet entered his brain. She stepped closer...up to within twenty feet. For a horrible moment she wasn't certain she could pull the trigger.

The light in the valley was now a bright gold, birds filled the morning with their song and closing her eyes, Clarisse tried to block out the bubbling sounds rising from Dale, from the torn remains of his lacerated throat. Instead, she recalled the previous morning when she had stood near this same spot, listening to the birds greeting the new day with her own heart filled with love for the moment. Briefly she recalled that feeling of happiness, and with a smile on her lips, her fingers pulled the trigger.

EURWICCAN

Introduction

Before we proceed further it would behoove me to take a few minutes to introduce myself. I am a witch. No, I do not ride on a broom or make stews out of bats or rats. I don't own a black cat...though I do love cats and have two of them...a tiger tom and a white and orange tom. Of course, they haven't been true toms since they were kittens. I am a Wiccan and I support others through the hurdles of life when they need a bit of assistance.

I live in Eureka Springs, Arkansas. If you've never been here, you have missed out and need to add it to your bucket list. It is, quite simply, as close to heaven as you can hope to get on this ball of rock we live on. I firmly believe it's why my magic is so effective. Who has not heard of the magnetic powers in Sedona, Arizona? Well, Eureka Springs has the same, or stronger, draw for some of us. You'll know when you get here if it has that power over you.

And what a power it is. It took me exactly forty-one and a half years almost to the day to arrive home. And that was a near miss, purely by chance and a suggestion from a dear friend. I was engaged and the wedding date was drawing near. We had six months to decide on a venue. Not that it was a typical wedding. It was not the first for either of us and we didn't feel the need to have a large elaborate ceremony. We were looking for small and intimate, intimate being the key word. That does not resonate with inclusiveness. My friend popped out one day with, "Why not Eureka Springs?"

"Eureka Springs?" I had never heard of it.

"Oh, yes. It was *the* wedding destination in the late 1800's, early 1900's."

"This is 2005," I responded a tad drily.

She just laughed and said, "Check it out. It's in northwest Arkansas."

So, I did. It was tucked into the very northwest corner of Arkansas in the Ozark Mountains. Having grown up in the mountains of southwestern Pennsylvania I instantly felt a pull. What I saw online sealed the deal and I proceeded with booking our wedding at a lovely old Victorian mansion in the heart of the small city nestled on its two mountainsides.

Our wedding date was two days before Christmas, December twenty-third. This is the off-season, and that might be a bit understated, for Eureka Springs. Which consequently made it ideal and our wedding almost fairylike. The town was dressed up in Christmas finery, lights glowing in the cold winter dusk and the horse drawn carriage with its merry bells tinkled cheerfully through the old winding streets.

I'd grown accustomed to the straight roads of Dallas and the other metropolitan jungles I'd spent my adult life living in. The twisting, turning roads of the Ozark Mountains were nothing but sheer joy. Driving on straight roads pales in comparison and I confess that in my private heart I have a secret desire to drive NASCAR. The thrill of a big V8 pulling through the backend of a sharp mountain curve...well, that's just incomparable. But I digress.

As I said, our wedding was magical even if it did lack any family participation, much to my new mother-in-law's consternation. We only stayed two nights and headed home to be with family on Christmas day. Those two nights changed my life forever.

We found ourselves returning to Eureka Springs at least once a year. Three years later we were there for a weeklong vacation and had a new toy, our first GPS. Such freedom! Or so we thought at the time and it did not ever let us down when we were in Eureka Springs which is a good thing. We've learned since then that GPS and wireless devices can be less than dependable in mountains. On this trip we discovered Beaver Lake. I have traveled our country, from sea to shining sea. I was born on the Canadian border in New York, lived in Pennsylvania, Maryland, Florida, Georgia and Texas. I have visited Washington and down that coast to California. I've been to Alaska, the entire eastern seaboard and covered the interior through Nebraska and Kansas, Kentucky and Tennessee. In short, I've seen a lot of beautiful places. In all those travels I have never seen anything as pristine and naturally beautiful as this lake. And never has anything had the appeal or called to me as this gem of a city flanking the mountains has done.

As we drove that day and I glimpsed homes perched above the rocky shoreline with its limestone cliffs and an abundance of waterfalls I could not believe that anyone was so blessed to wake up every day to such beauty. I turned to my husband, exclaiming, "People live like this?"

He smiled; no words were necessary.

It was then the idea first occurred to me. "We could retire here," I ventured cautiously.

"We could," was his response. "I think we should explore a bit first before we jump into any decisions." He likes to think things through.

At that time, we were driving down a dirt road winding hazardously above the lake, which was a drop straight below us of about eighty feet. I am afraid of heights, but I don't recall any fear that day. Eventually the road left the lake and wound up the mountainside. We reached a gap in the trees and could see down to the sparkling blue water and a distant cove across the lake where several mountain humps converged and folded together. After this a sign boldly claimed that from this point forward was private property, do not trespass. We obligingly turned around and set our new GPS to take us back to our hotel.

So, more time passed. We lived in Dallas, spent the occasional week in Eureka Springs, and followed my husband's suggestion of exploring. We went to New Mexico, Arizona, Colorado and Utah…and always we ended up back in Eureka Springs. Finally, we grew serious. There was no longer any question. We had explored and we had no need to look further. Eureka Springs called, and we responded. We began referring to it as The Black Hole. It kept sucking us back.

First, we looked at homes. Now, I was anchored in Dallas with an excellent career. I was in no position to move at that time and we already had a mortgage strapped on our backs. We spent two trips looking at homes but never found that perfect place. At least not anything within our budget and I was unwilling to compromise in this area. It *had* to be perfect, simply put and nothing else would do.

Then, in the spring of 2012 we spent a week exploring undeveloped land on the lake. It was a rainy, foggy, cold week. Probably not the best week to be shopping for land but the conditions were ideal to see the land at its absolute best. Waterfalls abounded, redbud trees had a profusion of pink blossoms and the dog woods looked like puffs of cotton through the dense woods. We looked at property after property. I had scoured the internet and had a list of close to twenty-five different plots for us to look at.

After three days, we ventured to a new part of the lake we had never explored, the Big Clifty region. At the end of the damp third day, just as dusk was beginning to descend, we found It. Tucked down in a ravine, with a natural spring that runs year-round, and huge rock boulders throwing up shoulders to block wind and rain, was our perfect site.

Remember that GPS trip? That was five years before we bought the land we live on today. The year after we built the house, we went exploring. We found that road. We hadn't been able to find it again even though we had looked for it. We had never taken notice of the roads we took, the twists, the turns…we just went that day and trusted the GPS to get us back. Well, as I said, we found that road a year later. That gap? Well, it's directly across from the cove we built on. In the winter, with no leaves, you can spot our house now with a pair of binoculars.

Is Eureka Springs a black hole that pulls some of us inexorably into her arms and never lets us go? Yes. I firmly believe this. And as many Eurekan's have discovered, it comes at a cost. If you pay the price, the reward is rich. Perhaps not materially so, but in ways that cannot be measured on such a mundane scale as money.

That excellent career? Gone within three and a half years of our move. No one would ever have imagined that I would become a practicing Wiccan, least of all myself. I had always been so practical, so dedicated to the career ladder I was arduously, yet successfully, climbing.

I have heard that pastors and preachers are called to their duty. I understand. I was called. I was called to Eureka Springs and slowly, once I proved my sticking power and that I could handle a bit of personal adversity, the powers and joys of this treasure in the Ozarks opened for me like a rose to the sun. Take some time to sit back, relax, and join me as I introduce our colorful citizens and life in our quirky, beautiful, historic city.

Mandy

I met Mandy at Hart's. Hart's is our local grocery store and has been here forever.

Mandy is how I think the woman in Rod Stewart's song *You're In My Heart* might look, right down to the Dutch accent. Mandy's may have been more German, I'm no judge when it comes to the difference. Mainly because I don't know if I've ever met anyone with a Dutch accent. We have an Amish community nearby and I've spoken with the women frequently at Walmart's, but they have American accents...no trace of Dutch. So, Mandy that resembles the song is indeed a big bosomed lady, and, as I said, she has a German/Dutch accent. Only Mandy is about forty years senior to the lady in Rod's song, I'm fairly certain. She is by no means a magnet for men as more than her bosom is big. Most of Mandy is big. Including her application of makeup. All of which is her subconscious need to hide the real Mandy behind an audacious mask. I figured this out within the first five seconds of exchanging hellos as we passed in the cereal aisle.

I also instantly noticed the extreme redness of her eyes. We're talking extremely bloodshot eyes. Not strangle me bad but not far from it, either. She was either suffering from severe allergies or was stoned out of her mind. I tended to think it was the first versus the latter. She just didn't have a stoner look to her.

Not that you could tell by her mode of dress. She wore a frilly skirt that ended just above a chubby knee. A pair of hose were pulled above the knee and tied off with long sheer scarves that fluttered down the back of her largish calves to her ankles only slightly overflowing the granny boots on her feet.

The T-strap camisole hugged her big bosom while a sheer drape of some sort hung over her shoulders enveloping her from neck to mid-booty. And what a booty! Large suffices. A big floppy hat over puffed bottle-blond hair perfected the look. And yet, she didn't look bad. Different, certainly…but in her own way she pulled it off. She knew how to work bling.

As I continued down the aisle in my direction and she in hers I considered she could also have been suffering from an infection from contact lenses. She had been wearing glasses that tended to magnify the blue irises and iridescently shaded blue eyelids behind the lenses, along with the bright red corneas. I recalled when I'd gotten my first infection from improperly cleaned contact lenses when I'd been a teenager. At the time, I'd worked as a waitress in a Greek restaurant near the square in our small hometown. I remember the owner, a middle-aged short man from Greece that we all called Papa. One day after I'd been working for him for about a week, and I've got this flaming eye infection but stubbornly insisted on wearing the contacts causing the problem, he sits me down at his table in the corner of the dining room. He reaches across and pats my hand and awkwardly states, in his thick Greek accent, "You have trouble…you know…. trouble with…. hmmm…. say with the drugs…. hmmm…. well, you canna always talk to Papa. Hmmm. OK?"

I remember sitting stunned and not understanding why he was saying this to me. I stammered, "Sure…. ok, sure. If that's ever an issue, I'll do that. Thanks, Papa."

His eyes seemed to search mine for an eternity and then with a deep sigh, and a dismissive wave he said, "OK. Enough we talk."

So, maybe Mandy had an allergy *and* an eye infection. Not my concern anyway. I rounded the cereal aisle into the candy and medicine aisle…and sure enough, there's Mandy putting a box of allergy pills in her cart beside a large bottle of eye drops. This time our smiles were a bit more exaggerated and we each gave that nervous little laugh you feel obliged to give when you realize you are on alternating courses with someone in a grocery store. You know what I mean. Now, we pass many people in a grocery store and most of them we don't really take notice of. But once you meet someone in every aisle at about the same location after two aisles you know you're on a course with this person.

I don't believe in coincidences. I try to remain vigilant to their occurrences and watch for the opportunity they represent. Mandy was someone I was supposed to meet. By the time we reached the soup and general-purpose aisle, I was prepared. I stopped beside Mandy next to the chicken and beef broths and said, "How long have you been suffering with allergies?"

She blinked, a little taken aback by my boldness, and then said with perfect calmness, "As long as I can remember, but it's been especially bad this summer."

I pulled my checkbook out and flipped to the calendar on the back of the register. "Hmmm," I mused. "Monday, October second, would be best."

"Excuse me?" She was clearly puzzled, her head cocked towards her left shoulder as she studied me.

I returned her gaze and replied, "If you want to try something that may bring you some relief and doesn't require putting potentially harmful chemicals into your body, I may know a way to help."

"Oh." Her response was flat and colored now with a bit of suspicion.

I smiled, in what I hoped was a warm and welcoming manner and stuck out my right hand. "I'm Polly. Polly Lewis."

She took my hand, pumped once with a firm grip, and released. "Mandy. Mandy Easton."

I reached back into my purse and pulled out a business card. "I have a salon on Spring Street just before you get to Mountain. On the left as you go up. I'm on the second floor in a loft. The door on Spring Street has *Pollyana* stenciled on it. Stop by for a cup of coffee or tea. I've got some fabulous green and jasmine teas. No charge." I smiled warmly. "I just couldn't help but notice you were suffering," as my gaze swept her cart.

She nodded and her suspicious look changed to an assessing look. "'Tis true. I suffer." A statement plainly returned. She looked at the card now in her hand and then again at me. A firm nod. "OK. Maybe I stop by. Have a good day." And she was on her way.

That was on Saturday, September sixteenth. On Thursday, September twenty-first, Mandy appeared in the doorway of my salon. My salon occupies the entire second floor of a narrow brick building midway up the incline after the righthand dogleg Spring Street takes before it reaches Mountain Street. The front half, where clients first enter from the dark alcove at the head of the stairs, is set up as a traditional hair salon. I have excellent light flooding into this half from the two east facing windows over Spring. There is also a narrow glass door that lets onto an equally narrow patio with ornate metal railing which serves as a cover for the shop below and pedestrians that stroll up and down gazing into our many boutiques and specialty shops. I have an abundance of plants filling as much of the narrow space as practicable and still be able to move around. More hang from brackets mounted into the side of the building.

When Mandy appeared, I was in the middle of blow drying a customer's hair and I paused to smile brightly and say, "Good morning, Mandy!"

She smiled back and said, "Morning."

I indicated the group of chairs arranged in a small circle where clients can sit while they wait and said, "I'll be with you in a bit if you don't mind waiting."

She nodded and moved to take a seat, picking up a magazine to occupy her while she waited.

I turned my attention back to the silky blue strands I was blowing dry. The blue hair belonged to my best friend Denise. Her natural hair color is an ethereal platinum blonde. She has the color so many women strive to attain from a bottle but only the ones born to it ever really achieve it. And it only really looks good on them as they always seem to have that golden skin tone that offsets it perfectly. For reasons I've never really understood Denise persists in shading her gorgeous hair into bizarre colors. I blame it on myself. When we were younger, she used the traditional permanent dyes, or semi-permanent, and the harsh chemicals would damage her hair over time. I wise-cracked one day that she could do like the kids at Halloween and use powdered drink mixes which would wash out safely after a short while. And here we are.

Denise is, simply put, stunningly gorgeous. She has blue eyes. Only saying blue doesn't nearly begin to describe or do them justice. I think of them as the Blue of Many Hues. I've seen them turn a stormy, angry ocean gray of a harsh winter's day and I've also seen them turn a deep, dark blue of a perfectly cloudless summer day when the sun is so hot and the sky so blue it's hard to look at. Typically, they're somewhere in between…an indeterminate gray that is deep blue if you look into them long enough. Denise allows plenty of opportunity to look into them long enough. She has a very direct gaze and gives her full attention to anyone she is conversing with. I've watched in social settings and most people are uncomfortable with such a direct and piercing stare and will typically look away. I don't. I know Denise and she's not trying to intimidate…she's just trying to show her interest.

At thirty-five Denise has a knock-out, absolutely amazing, stop-you-in-your-tracks-for-a-second-look figure. She knows it and clothes it to do it justice. I don't mean she knows it in a vain way because there is nothing about Denise that is vain. In fact, she's almost naïve in her basic goodness.

Right now, she had her eyes glued to my face in the mirror and her delicate lightly colored eyebrows raised inquisitively. "So, go on," she urged in her slightly husky, deep voice which is always a bit surprising coming from such a slight and wraithlike figure, "What happened?"

I had been in the middle of telling her about my horror movie episode first thing that morning. "So, I had just applied conditioner to my hair and worked it in, and was pinning it up, when I sense movement. Now, remember, Scott left to go do some work for the neighbors so I'm all alone in the house. It immediately occurred to me that I hadn't locked the front door before coming down to take my shower."

This caused Denise to frown at me and shake her head, which pulled the neon colored hair out of my hands and I had to start that strand over. I tapped her head lightly with the brush. "No moving!" I admonished. She giggled and I continued, "So, here I am in the shower and I look over and the shower curtain is being twitched to the side about half way down."

Denise gasped, "No!"

I nodded, "Oh yes. My first thought is Scott's come back and he's playing one of his jokes on me. So, I call out, 'Scott, is that you?' Well…" and I pause for full effect and meet her gaze in the mirror, "Well…silence…and another twitch of the curtain. Now I'm scared. I know it's not Scott."

"Oh, I think I'd've had a heart attack right then and there!" Denise breathed.

"Well, the mystery was quickly solved when a black nose and white muzzle made an appearance finally in the shower. It was Brandy."

"Oh, how funny!" Denise laughed. "Oh, I would have loved to see your face when that curtain first moved! I'll bet that was priceless!"

"Oh, sure, priceless!" I faked indignation. "I was terrified!" I spun her chair around, whipping off the protective drape as I did so. *Oh, my!* I thought with some amazement as my eyes caught the dual image captured in the mirror now behind Denise. There sat Denise in a smart-looking two-piece linen suit in a light gray with a tight black polka dot pattern, and over her shoulder was Mandy, flipping through the pages of the magazine, in an off-white knee length kaftan covered in large black polka dots over black tights. Denise wore fashionable three-inch black suede pumps while Mandy had on gaudy rhinestone sandals with a short heel. "I guess I missed the message," I chirped thoughtlessly.

Denise looked at me in puzzlement and the susurration of the flipping magazine pages paused as Mandy looked up quizzically. "Polka dots," I replied to the unspoken question from them both. "You're both wearing polka dots." I smiled lamely at them. I had thrown on a simple purple silk blouse over black slacks with sensible flat ballet slippers with a nice inner support for a long day on my feet. Or that was my wishful thinking, anyway. The truth was that I had a pretty light schedule. Thursdays aren't my busiest day. My thick, black hair was pulled back into a casual ponytail that cascaded down my back in riotous curls.

"Denise, meet Mandy!" I said to Denise and grandly waved a bow to Mandy. "Mandy, meet Denise!" Reversing the same gestures.

They smiled at each other and simultaneously exchanged, "Hello" and then laughed to cover the awkward moment. "Well," Denise said, breaking the suddenly over loud silence, "I need to get the store opened." She rose, gave me a quick peck on the check and shoved some bills in my hand before I could stop her. And just as quickly she was across the salon and opening the outer door. Turning, she called over her shoulder, "Let me know what you're doing Saturday afternoon. I was thinking of taking *Esmerelda* out for an evening lake tour if you and Scott want to tag along. I could swing by your cove and pick you up."

"That sounds heavenly," I said with real feeling. It did, too. I reflected that I really hadn't had a chance to enjoy the lake as much this summer as I usually did. "I'll talk to Scott tonight and call you tomorrow sometime."

"Sounds good." And she was gone.

I followed her to the door and thumbed the deadbolt, locking the door behind her, and flipped the Open sign to Closed. I turned to Mandy and smiled cheerfully, "Cup of tea?"

She frowned a bit at the locked door but slowly nodded and added a little hesitantly, "Sure."

I smiled and reassured her. "I have a small kitchenette in the back, and I don't want anyone to wander in while we chat. I don't have any appointments until later this afternoon, so I'll just switch off the sign downstairs and we should be undisturbed." I suited actions to words, crossing to my small appointment desk and used my app on my phone to deactivate the Open sign on the lower door.

I led Mandy through the back of the studio, and we entered my small private domain. I proceeded to the kitchen nook while Mandy took a seat at the table where she could face me. She gazed around the room while I prepared our tea.

"This is a lovely space," she said.

I nodded and sighed contentedly as I looked around the room. It is a lovely space. The ceilings are higher than average at ten feet with the ceiling itself being a very decorative tin burnished with age. Intricate crown molding joined the ceiling elegantly to the walls which were a creamy just off-white. The floor is wood and darkened with age but lustrous and shiny in the wonderful light flooding through the tall windows. I had installed a small kitchen space in the far back corner where a smaller window over the sink looked out over the rock bluff the building snugged up against. Three larger windows lined up along this back wall creating a large view of the rock formation. Small ferns and tiny wild flowers grew in the crevices and it was an enchanting micro world I never tired of looking at. I have a very small balcony accessed by a door between the kitchen space and the window wall and I have a bird feeder hung from the corner eave. I once saw a male Painted Bunting and his colors were so vivid in the eternally shaded space it was almost surreal. The rest of the space is a relaxed living area with a small table where I have three chairs across from a small sofa and love seat in front of an old fireplace which has since been blocked up. The original mantle and marble casing remained and added a wonderful warmth to the space.

I carried the two cups of tea to the table and took the seat across from Mandy. The warm fragrance of the brewed rooibos tea, with a touch of licorice root lending an earthy aroma, wafted on the gently rising steam.

She sniffed inquisitively at the cup and then arched a brow at me. "What is this?" she asked.

"Something that will help to soothe your allergies, I think. It's rooibos tea and I added a sliver of licorice root. Rooibos tea is known to block histamines and the licorice root relieves breathing passages." I inhaled deeply through my nose, demonstrating with a smile.

Mandy nodded and took a sip of the hot beverage, placing the tea diffuser ball on the saucer. She nodded approvingly as she set her cup back down. "It is very good. Perhaps you could share the recipe? Or tell me where I can get some?"

I nodded, "Of course. I'll give you some to take home. If you drink two cups a day I think it will help to relieve a lot of your symptoms. Green tea is also good. Especially if you're already suffering from the effects. It can really relieve watery eyes and sneezing."

Mandy drank more of her tea, her eyes roaming the surface of the table and settling on the deck of tarot cards stacked neatly at my right hand. She turned her gaze to me. "You read cards?"

I took a sip of my own tea, and nodded, "I do."

"Hmmm." She said and then added, "I had mine read once. A long time ago."

"Was it helpful?" I asked.

She gave a small shrug. "Maybe. At the time it did seem to fit what I was going through."

I picked up the deck and shuffled the cards idly. "Would you like me to read yours now?"

She smiled and waved her left hand casually in the air, "Bah. No one believes that stuff, do they?"

It was my turn to shrug. "It depends, I suppose. I've found them to be quite accurate at times. I've seen them offer my clients suggestions that have given them good results." I continued shuffling the cards. "It depends very much on the person and whether or not they are receptive." My eyes rose and met hers directly.

I liked the responding challenge in her unswerving gaze as she said, "Okay."

I neatened the deck and handed it to her, "Go ahead and loosely shuffle these. If there is something you want answers to, think about that situation. Try to begin to think of a question you would like answered." While she shuffled, I rose and went back into the kitchen, turning on a small oil burner on the granite countertop. Then I lit a small white votive candle and carried it back to the table with me. I set it off to my left-hand side, between us, and held out my hand for the cards. As Mandy laid the deck on my open palm, I told her, "Go ahead and cut the deck."

She hesitated, her hand floating inches above mine, and then she selected the top third of the deck and I closed mine around the rest, tucking the cards she handed me under the bottom. "Have you thought of a question?" I asked her.

She nodded pensively, her eyes watching the cards. Apparently, she was reluctant to share her question, so I continued, "I'm going to do a star spread for you. It should highlight both inner and outer influences in your life right now. It should help you to see the potential inherent or the various possibilities."

"Okay," she said, leaning forward a little and I detected curiosity.

I began to lay the cards out in the star spread pattern. I laid the first card in front of Mandy at the six o'clock position assuming my seat was twelve o-clock. Card two went at the four while card three went to seven. I laid the fourth card directly in the center, the fifth card at the two o'clock position, sixth at ten and the final card at twelve. I looked at the seven cards I had laid out and looked back at Mandy.

I was surprised to see the alarm clearly written in her eyes. "What is it?" I asked.

"The Devil!" she whispered.

"Oh!" I smiled in what I hoped was a reassuring manner. "Not to worry, it's in a good spot. Here, let's go through this and I'll explain what each card is representing. We'll start here with the Five of Coins." I tapped the card immediately in front of her. "This card represents the root of the matter. I'm not sure what your question was but I'd guess it was related to money." I paused, and she gave a small affirmative nod. "This card tells me that you feel like something is lacking maybe, or that perhaps you've over extended yourself. It also tells me that this fear is *not* grounded in reality."

I saw hope spring into her eyes, and I smiled warmly at her. "This card also has an underlying message that you need to take care of yourself." I nodded at the cup of tea. "Drinking that is a good first step." I moved my gaze to the second card, the one resting at the four o'clock position. I tapped it. "This card is a clue to what you're dealing with emotionally. You have an Eight of Cups here." I frowned a little and studied her face again, looking deeply into her eyes. "You've outgrown something. You're ready to move on…Or you're starting a new venture. Is that it? Are you having some financial worries, afraid you'll lose it all…because you're starting something new?" I looked back down at the table and took in the third card at the seven o'clock position, the Seven of Swords.

"Interesting," I murmured. "This card suggests you need to find a roundabout way of doing this…it would be best not to tackle this head on. It will take patience and a willingness to persevere." I met Mandy's gaze again. She smiled determinedly and gave a little nod.

I turned back now to The Devil, sitting in the middle at the fourth spot. "It seems that the real root of the problem is that you have blockages hindering your growth but you're ready to deal with them now." I tapped the Seven of Swords again. "Remember that I said you'd need patience?" She nodded, and I continued, "Because you need to deal with your own inner demons before you move forward with this." And here I tapped card number two, the Eight of Cups and the new venture it seemed to indicate.

Then I moved on to The Sun, sitting at two o'clock in the fifth card spot. "Yes, that would explain the sense of loss I feel in the Five of Coins at the first spot. You have a lot of hope riding on this. It means an awful lot to you, whatever it is."

Next, I looked at the Seven of Wands in the sixth position at ten o'clock and smiled. "But as I already suspected you're more than capable of dealing with this. You've got the willpower and while it won't be easy, you have what it takes to succeed. And, is if you needed further proof..." and I tapped the Wheel of Fortune card sitting at the top in the twelve o'clock spot. "This card position in this reading represents the possible outcome of your question. This card, the Wheel of Fortune, indicates a new start...a new beginning. One chapter is ending, a new one starting." I finished and leaned back, sipping from my cup and studying the cards spread between us. It was amazing how closely the various cards seemed to be related and clearly told a message. I wondered again what Mandy's question may have been. She was obviously dealing with some situation that had the potential to really impact her life.

Mandy finished her tea and set her cup firmly back in the saucer. "Very good," she said, nodding with satisfaction. "A good reading. Now," and she paused while she pulled her cell phone out of her purse and I watched her fingers move across the screen, "You said something the other day about Monday, October second."

"Oh! Yes!" I shuffled the tarot cards back together and returned them to their sleeve, pulling my appointment book over and flipping to the next month. "Let's see, I penciled you in for that morning..." I flipped to the page for October and sure enough, I'd penciled Mandy in for the morning of Tuesday, October second. "October second is the start of the last phase of the waning moon."

Mandy arched a manicured eyebrow in what I suspected was the first indication of skepticism. I've become accustomed to that pattern by now. Modern women are not as close to the ancient knowledge that was once universally shared and passed down, generation to generation, the way I learned from my mother and my grandmother. I decided to try a different tactic. "Have you ever read *The Farmer's Almanac*?"

Mandy gave a half shrug, "Sure. I've seen copies and have looked through them before."

"Well, historically farmers have followed the phases of the moon to guide them on when to plant crops, sow seeds, to ensure a successful harvest. *The Farmer's Almanac* has simplified this by publishing a Best Days Calendar. You can find it in the printed *Almanac* or locate it online. They've expanded the calendar to include all sorts of things...like the best day to quit smoking...and then lists the dates for whatever topic you're interested in. All of this is actually based on the phases of the moon."

Mandy had started nodding when I mentioned farmers. "Yes, yes. I have heard of such. I did not know it was used outside of farming."

I couldn't suppress a chuckle. "It's used in farming today, but it had much broader uses before we became so civilized."

"Okay," she replied, "And what then is October second good for?"

"Well, it's a good day to get rid of your allergies! Or at least make the effort. Between the tea and a small…" I wasn't sure how to proceed with Mandy, words like *spell* and *ritual* seemed like poor choices. "I know of a cure I learned from my grandmother. Before modern technology and science and medicine, healers relied on what nature provided and as you know in some cultures healer and spiritual guides were often one and the same. For example, Native American Shamans…they cared for the spiritual as well as the physical well-being of the members of their tribe."

Mandy nodded but I again sensed skepticism. *Oh, well,* I thought to myself, *it's usually easier once the horse drinks the water.* I plunged onward. "Rather than go through it all here could you possibly meet me at East Mountain Overlook Monday morning? Perhaps at around nine o'clock? It will be far easier to explain as we go through the steps and I'd like you to keep an open mind. A receptive and open mind is critical for any real change in our lives."

Mandy glanced at the pack of tarot cards, gave a small shrug and nodded. "Okay. At the Overlook on Monday, nine o'clock. I'll be there." With this announcement she finished off the last of her tea and stood up. "The tea was very good." She stated.

"Oh, wait a moment and I'll give you some to take home." I quickly placed a handful of rooibos tea bags and a small packet of sliced licorice root in a little tin container which I handed to her. "You can get both the tea and the licorice root online. This should be enough for about a week. Two cups a day would be ideal. Once you achieve some relief with your sinuses you can probably eliminate the licorice root."

She accepted the tin and smiled. "Thank you. What do I owe you?"

"Owe?" I was puzzled. "You don't owe me anything, Mandy."

"Oh…well, the reading…?"

I smiled and shook my head. "No charge. I hope it was helpful for you."

She nodded resolutely and turned back to the door leading out to the salon. "Well, I think so, yes. I will see you Monday morning. Two weeks. October second."

That Monday ended up being a cloudy morning with high humidity and temperatures unusually high, already creeping past the mid-sixties at eight o'clock, as I pulled into the parking area beside East Mountain Overlook. I had arrived early so I could set things up before Mandy arrived. I carried my small bag of supplies over to the rock wall facing The Crescent Hotel on the crest of the opposite mountain and settled in to wait for Mandy. I could hear the early sounds of the city stirring to life, traffic moving up and down Main and Spring Streets. Birds were active in the tree canopy, filling the overcast morning with a bright cheer defying the absent sun. I heard the crunch of tires on gravel and turned to see a smart white Subaru wagon pull in beside my Jeep Liberty.

Mandy emerged and her entire demeanor seemed to have changed. Her hair was pulled back stylishly and simply in an attractive arrangement that framed her face nicely. Her eyes, I was pleased to see, were no longer bloodshot. With clear corneas the beautiful cornflower blue of her eyes was more evident, and I saw real beauty in her gaze. The bright makeup was absent, and she was instead tastefully yet very mutely made up with natural tones that warmly accentuated her features. She smiled almost shyly as she joined me under the pavilion.

"I wish it would go ahead and rain, yes? This humidity…bah!"

I smiled, "Yes. It's dreary enough. It does seem though that we may have the perfect conditions for a beautiful fall this year. That cooler weather and rain in September…though I know it's been hard on allergy sufferers these past couple of weeks when it warmed back up." I looked at her inquisitively. "How have your allergies been? Your eyes look ever so much better!"

She smiled broadly. "The tea is a miracle! I have been feeling so much better…a little trouble still, yes…but not so bad, not nearly so bad."

I smiled in response and patted the bag on the rock wall beside me. "Well, I hope this will help you let go of that last little bit. Now, it may seem silly what I'm going to do but I really need you to try to have confidence that it will work. If you can believe in it, if you really want success, then all you need do is have faith. Are you willing to try and have faith with me?"

She shrugged and nodded, "Yes."

I nodded and opened the bag. First, I removed a helium balloon which I handed to Mandy. I took out a strip of paper, two pens and a small yellow candle. I lit the candle and set it on the rock wall facing north out of the pavilion. I laid the strip of paper on the ledge between us just beside where I'd set the candle and handed her the first pen. "Write your name and the words 'Illness Be Gone'. Write it anywhere on the paper."

She took the pen, removed the cap and bent to write her name, pulling back in surprise when she couldn't see what she had written. She looked at me quizzically and I smiled. "It's white ink."

"Oh," she breathed and bent to finish writing her name and the words I'd given her. Then she straightened up and handed me back the pen. I gave her the second pen and instructed her, "Now, draw a tree or a plant or flower, maybe a bird or a butterfly…draw over your name and the words you just wrote."

Mandy took the pen with green ink and bent to follow my directions. While she drew, I spoke quietly, "Grow strong, tall as the trees, be free as a bird." I kept repeating the words until she straightened, capping the green pen and handing it back. She had drawn a beautiful green Luna moth in the center of the paper strip. I smiled tenderly and taking the strip of paper ran the cord attached to the balloon through the hole I'd punched earlier. I handed her the balloon and then placed my hands around hers. Together we held the balloon out of the pavilion until it caught the slight breeze that was blowing from the south, pulling the balloon towards the north and away from us, the candle reflecting gold in the silver mylar of the balloon with Well Wishes cheerfully stenciled on its side. "Now," I said, my eyes catching and holding hers, "Repeat those words with me: Grow strong, tall as the trees, be free as a bird." I said it slowly and she tentatively joined me, her voice a bare whisper. We said it again, a little faster, her voice a little stronger…until finally she was saying it quickly and confidently and fervently. Suddenly, I released my hands from hers and told her, "Let go!" As her hands opened, freeing the balloon to the tugging wind, I enjoined, "Fly free as the birds!" Together we watched the balloon drift north as though following the highway to Missouri in the distant north.

After a few moments we both sighed, laughed nervously over the synchronicity and then smiled warmly at one another. I snuffed the candle and tucked it into the bag, ridiculously empty now with the candle and two pens rolling around.

"So," I chirped as cheerfully as I could to break the sudden tension, "Let's see if that helps!"

Mandy nodded and suddenly reached out, laying a hand on my left arm and stopping me in the action of pulling my keys from my purse. "I want to thank you," she said meaningfully. She waved her other hand in the direction the balloon had flown, "For this, for helping, yes…but mostly…for the reading."

I froze, not speaking but letting her talk, letting her continue. "It was so very true to what is happening right now for me," she continued, obviously distressed and uncomfortable but needing badly to share. "My life," and she paused, turning away from me and walking to the south side of the pavilion, facing into the mild breeze keeping the humidity from being unbearable.

"Go on," I urged gently, "Maybe I can help."

She laughed in a bitter way that twisted my heart a little in sympathy for the pain she was so obviously dealing with. "I have not always made good choices or good decisions." Her voice continued to hold a bitterness and I resisted the impulse to hug her and comfort her. Right now, she simply needed to talk, and I am a good listener. She talked for some time, sharing problems, battles with depression, low self-esteem. She suddenly had an opportunity…a real gift of a chance, to do something she had always wanted to do…own and run her own shop. But she was terrified of failure. Terrified she would lose everything.

Finally, after speaking for about ten minutes, she turned to me, large tears magnifying her beautiful eyes and with real passion said, "So, again! Thank you!" And she rushed to me, grasping me in a warm hug.

I hugged her back fiercely. "You are so very welcome," I whispered as she held me close. I could feel her frame trembling as she shed tears of relief. "You're going to be fine, Mandy."

Finally, she calmed and pulled away. I grasped her shoulders and held her firmly. "You have a friend now, okay?" I implored, holding her eyes with my own. "I want you to stop by *Pollyana* and have tea with me. It can get lonely there sometimes," I smiled ruefully.

She smiled back and I saw the real Mandy, the kind and warm, caring person not hiding behind layers of masks and I saw she was a beautiful woman. I'm sure we'll be hearing more from Mandy in the future, for now I was content to know that I had helped her.

HEAT

The air was still, heavy. The heat was like another presence filling the interior of the small mobile home. Pressing down…its weight making it hard to breathe. I could feel the beads of sweat swelling along my hairline…itching and tickling.

"Get me 'nother beer, why don'cha?" and he dangled the empty long neck from his right hand, hanging over the side of his armchair. He lowered his left leg to the floor, spreading his legs wide so the hot blast of air stirred up by the fan could reach his testicles in the loose boxer shorts he wore. His left hand helped the direction of air flow a bit by pulling strategically at the wad of material between his legs. His fat dome of a pink stomach rose, the almost white hair catching the light from the window across the room. The cree of crickets almost drowning out the television.

I delayed, not wanting to move in the oppressive heat.

"Hey!" A bark.

I rose. He was known to bite.

I shuffled across the space to the shabby kitchen with its olive green turning brown seventies model refrigerator. The ice box was practically useless with thickly crusted ice liberally coating the interior and fuzzing the few packages that could be crammed into the space. One of these days I'd get around to defrosting it.

I wanted to ask about that air conditioner. I took another long neck out of the fridge…we had plenty of those, I noticed…and popped the top with the church key stuck to the door with a magnet. I shuffled back and placed it in his waiting beefy hand.

I sat back down on the end of the couch, slouching as deep into the corner as I could fit…my legs drawn up close even though it made the heat intolerable. Closed off…closed in. My safe position, my safe spot.

What was I thinking? I'd been doing that lately. Forget what I'd been thinking.

My eyes wandered over the TV screen, like I was watching…but I wasn't. Secretly, I wasn't watching. He didn't know that. He didn't really know everything…like he thought he did. He thought he knew…if he really knew…but no, I wasn't going to think about that. I'd promised myself.

If only it wasn't so hot. The air conditioner. That's what I was thinking! I brightened briefly. It was like that when you found a lost thought. I imagined that's how seeing an old friend might feel. I didn't have any old friends. I remembered that I wanted to ask him about the air conditioner, but I didn't think it was a good idea. I shot him a furtive glance as I reached for my slippery glass of ice water sitting in a puddle on the scarred surface of the coffee table.

His round pink face, stubbled with white hair, glistening wetly in the gleam of light from the window…the frown line between the small beady eyes. Those eyes fixed on the television screen. He should be blind I thought. For a moment I drifted into a pleasant day dream…

He's sitting in the same chair only he's helpless…he's blind…he's completely dependent on me now. I would be able to elude him…he'd never find me if he was blind…

"You see something interestin'?" the face sneered.

I looked away hurriedly. It was not good to get caught. That would mean at least a thirty minute no move penalty. If I could sit perfectly still for thirty minutes without drawing his attention, or until he got up to go to the bathroom, then we could put this behind us. For now, it wasn't safe to do anything. I felt the first pressure of needing to go to the bathroom.

Wonderful, I thought bitterly. Shutting down the thought, ignoring the impulse, clenching my legs tighter. I drifted into my daydream. Where was I? Oh, yes, the air conditioner. I would ask him…

"Have you checked the fuse? I remember once it was the fuse…" I allowed my voice to drift off, not completing the sentence, my eyes catching the look of him. He'd gone still in the chair. It reminded me of a time when I was a teenager…

I was with a couple of friends and we went to pick up another friend who lived in this row of townhouses. We pulled up and I jumped out of the cab of the pick-up we were in to go up to the house when this dog came from out of nowhere. Just all at once there's this dog right in front of me…snarling.

He was ugly, yellow and big. Not at all scrawny. You know, you always hear how the dog was snarling and scrawny…but this dog wasn't scrawny. His muzzle was right at my lower stomach. I had this horrible vision of him leaping forward. Those jaws gaping and biting, burrowing into my soft stomach, ripping through the tender muscles and spilling the deadly contents of my intestines into my body. I'd die an agonizing death.

That dog had been all stiff and still, a low steady rumble coming from the muscular chest,eyes never leaving mine…and that's what he reminded me of. All stiff and still, and I knew what would come next. Only this time, no one would be there to grab the collar

No, I wouldn't ask about the air conditioner. In a while, a few more hours, the sun would fall below the line of roofs across the street and we'd get a little respite from the direct glare. Maybe there'd be a breeze.

I pulled the sticky cotton T-shirt away from my body. Seeking any draft, any current of air, for relief.

"Whyn't chu take it off? You'd be cooler," Another sneer, a swig from the beer.

I knew what was wrong with the air conditioner. I remember now that he'd told me it was the relay switch. Damned ants shorted out the relay switch. We couldn't afford the repair. Couple of hundred bucks total. But he had a case of beer in the fridge. Walked in the door with the beer. Already had three empties and three more long necks had joined those first three…like some kind of strange multiplying object mysteriously doubling. Only there was no mystery, and before the night was over, I expected they would double again. There was money for that. And money for the lottery tickets he bought, but never collected on.

I'd bought some poison for the ants. It was in a plastic container sitting on the end of the kitchen counter. Along with all the other clutter and detritus that seemed to collect on the end of the counter. There was a haphazard pile of junk mail and catalogs. He loved to go through them and there were countless times he'd ordered the junk. And the debts piled up. You'd think they'd stop sending him junk mail and catalogs for stuff.

There was a little plastic bubble box of nails. I had no idea what they were for. I'm not even sure we had a hammer. There was some loose grass trimmer line from his failed attempt to fix the weed eater over a month ago. Under the line was the last notice from the trailer park threatening a fine if we didn't clean up the tiny spot they deemed a yard. It had one scraggly looking holly bush that looked like it had mange and a few straggles of Johnson grass that managed to grow exceptionally tall in such adverse conditions. The ducks from the local pond liked to come over and shit on the hard-packed dirt that passed for the remainder of a yard.

I'd tried to make the place pretty when we first moved in, but the plastic flowers I'd stuck in the ground had all faded to a non-color shade of white. They looked like odd pieces of metal sticking up out of the dirt…which is what they were, I guess. I kept a small and scraggly garden alive in the back, producing withered and tiny produce. A couple of puny broccolis had been ready to pick, otherwise they'd bolt by next week in this heat. They sat in the colander in the sink. Beside them was a small bowl of mushrooms.

I had bought the ant poison when he told me about the relay switch. He'd laughed at me. It had been one of the good nights. He hadn't turned ugly.

He just laughed, saying, "You're a little late, ain'tcha? That ain't going to fix the air conditioner, now is it?"

I'd put my hands on my hips and replied fiercely, "No, it won't, but it'll kill the God damned ants, at least!"

That had made him laugh even harder. He even got up and got his own beer, he was so tickled.

I had to hide a smile behind a sip of water. It was so hard sometimes to hold my laughter inside. I didn't think he'd see the humor though. I wasn't even sure now what had been so amusing. But that didn't make any sense did it?

My head was starting to hurt. I had to stop thinking. The heat...it was weighing me down.

I imagined having a conversation with Heat. Heat would be a big old huge bear of a man. He'd be so big he wouldn't be able to walk...he'd just sort of roll along. With great overlapping folds of fat...all drenched and dripping in sweat. You'd smell him coming. He'd reek.

"Why don't you just go away?" I'd ask Heat.

"Why?" he'd reply, and his voice would be deep and rumble.

"Because you aren't wanted." I'd reply, feeling brave, turning my chin up to look down at him better.

"You'd rather be Cold?" he taunted.

I debated, remembering Cold. I was on intimate terms with Cold. Cold could be worse than Heat. I recalled a winter, was it five years ago now? There had been snow on the ground...maybe as much as a foot, drifts even larger...and the temperature had plummeted at night down into the teens. I couldn't remember now what had started it but as usual he had been drinking steadily all day and was well into a drunken state by eight o'clock on that bitterly cold night. I had done something...I always did, didn't I, I thought bitterly. Whatever offense I had done him, whatever crime I had committed, it had resulted in him shoving me viciously out the trailer door and down the short flight of concrete steps. No coat, just a pair of moccasin slippers on my feet. He had slammed and locked the door behind me.

It had not taken more than five minutes for me to begin shivering violently. I couldn't even get into the run-down old Century station wagon. He kept it locked up even though the most hard-up of criminals wouldn't look twice at it. Who would ever think there was anything valuable in the old, turd brown rust bucket let alone want to take it for a joy ride?

I had pounded on the door, pleading, "Please...let me in! I can't bear it out here!"

Through the metal door I had heard his response, "Shut your trap, woman." And then I had heard the blare of the TV as he turned the volume up to drown me out.

I had no one to turn to. No door in this neighborhood would be opened for me. I had no friends in this shanty park of decrepit trailers. Oh, I knew the couple in the big doublewide two streets over. They supplied him with his reefer. Something else he managed to afford. More important than the relay switch for the air conditioner.

I was usually his mule. Trudging over with a grimy twenty shoved in my pocket to purchase whatever the man would give me. And he would complain with whatever I brought back.

"Was a time a twenty-dollar bill could buy you a whole ounce," he'd grumble. "Why, you could buy nickel bags for five bucks. Why else would you call 'em nickel bags? I should go over there and have a word with him. He ripped you off. You're too damned dumb to even know it."

It didn't matter that I'd had to beg for the small bit I'd gotten. The thin twist of a man grudgingly giving me two buds for the twenty while his fat slob of a wife slept on the couch, her twat on full display with her legs spread lewdly.

I tried to tell him, "It was all he would give me…" but before I could get further his ham of a fist smashed against the side of my head, knocking me to my knees.

As I knelt on the dirty floor, my ears ringing, he had laughed briefly and then sat on the couch twisting a joint from one of the buds. The joint rolled, he leaned back and inhaled deeply, then coughed harshly as he expelled a great plume of smoke. "Damn, this is shit weed! I wouldn't even give five bucks for this."

I had no one to turn to so I had crouched on the bottom step, trying to draw into myself and conserve body heat, shivering uncontrollably. I had no idea how long I was out there before I heard the door open behind me and he said harshly, "Get your ass in here." My toes and fingers hurt horribly once they began to thaw out. I suspect I came close to having frostbite that bitter night.

No, I wasn't at all sure I'd prefer Cold over Heat. And what did it really matter? Today was only August third. It would be at least September before there was any hope of cooler weather. At least for now, Heat was here to stay.

The pressure to pee came back fiercely and I knew I couldn't delay any longer. I didn't want to risk another bladder infection and didn't have any cranberry juice to prevent one. So, trying to be as invisible as possible, I rose from the couch and trudged down the short hall to the ugly yellow and orange colored bathroom with its festering commode. Cockroaches scrambled as I flicked on the weak florescent over the sink.

After relieving myself I stood for a minute looking at the haggard reflection in the fly speckled mirror. I had once been pretty. Not beautiful, but passably pretty. The years had not been kind. Deep grooves lined my forehead horizontally and companion grooves framed my full lips. My lips were too full, or at least I thought they were. I could not understand the current trend of women injecting Botox into their lips when I so desperately wished that mine were less. Same with breasts. I had a heavy set, too heavy. At forty I was already feeling the onslaught of back pain, a harbinger of even greater discomfort as I grew older.

I was not a large woman. I have a diminutive height at just under five feet one inch. I always tried to claim that extra inch, but I was just shy of it. My large breasts made all of me look large. If I wore anything that accentuated my smaller waist, then my large breasts were even more emphasized, and I did not welcome the attention they drew.

My female doctor would ask me every year, "Have you considered a reduction? I'll bet you have back problems."

Each time I would laugh and reply, "No. I don't think that would go over too well."

Not to mention I couldn't afford anything like a reduction. My job at Circle K didn't include benefits and I wouldn't have even gotten the yearly exam except it was the only way I could continue to get birth control. Fortunately, Planned Parenthood provided the exam and the prescription at a minimal cost because of my low income.

It wasn't that I didn't want a baby. I would have loved to have a baby. But not in this life. I couldn't bear the thought of bringing a child into this hellhole. What future might a child have with him as its father? No, better to take the pills.

Bitterly I thought briefly about my sister. She had three children…two boys and one girl. I never got to see them. How old would they be now? The oldest would be about nineteen, I thought, and the youngest about thirteen. She'd had the two boys almost back to back, getting pregnant almost as soon as she'd recovered from the first. The girl had come along a few years later.

We didn't talk. I hadn't talked to my sister now in over twelve years. We'd had a falling out. Over him, naturally. In the end, it was always him.

I could see now how he had intentionally isolated me. Driving off any friends I'd had when we met, turning my own family against me. I'd been raised to believe that marriage was for life, for better or for worse, until death us do part. Well, and so it had been for worse…and now I must lie in the bed I'd made.

"What cha doin' back there? You fall in?" He chuckled at his own wit.

So original, I thought snidely. "Coming now…"

"Well, grab me 'nother beer while you're up. And what about dinner? I'm getting hungry."

Of course, he was. Watching TV was labor, bound to work up an appetite. That's all he did. He slept, drank beer, watched TV. Day in and day out. Smoking his joints, eating, doing nothing. Couldn't, or stated more honestly, wouldn't hold a job. No, the job of providing was left to me. And the pittance

I got barely paid rent and utilities, leaving scant else to buy food with. But I managed, buying meat when it was slashed down in price, usually just on the verge of spoiling. Getting those big logs of ground beef and then freezing them in smaller bags; cramming the small freezer space as best as possible. A poor man's diet, ground beef.

The thought now of standing over a hot stove in that hotter trailer was too daunting. What else could I do, though? An outdoor grill would be nice. I enjoyed stepping outside and smelling someone else's grill cooking some tasty barbecued chicken or steak, perhaps. We had no grill.

I would have no choice but to make the kitchen even more unbearable. I could turn on the exhaust fan over the stove to help draw the heat out, but that would be too noisy. Just best to get it over with even though I had absolutely no appetite. Who wanted to eat when it was this hot?

I trudged back down the dark hallway emerging into the brighter gloom of the living room. I would have to pass close to his chair if I went on through to the kitchen. I was almost past him when his foot rammed into my left hip, sending me crashing into the coffee table where I barely kept myself from falling.

"You forget sumthin'?" he snarled.

Hastily I grabbed the long neck from his hand and went into the kitchen, trying not to limp, my left buttock and hip hurting where he'd kicked me, my right palm felt bruised where I'd fallen against the edge of the table. I tossed the empty in the trash can and got another one from the refrigerator.

As I used the church key to pop the top, I heard the springs in his chair protesting, or sighing from relief, and the trailer trembled as he lurched to his feet. I froze in the act of opening the bottle, all senses alert to his movement. In my mind I pictured a mouse, aware of the cat sitting five feet away and poised to pounce. Who would be faster today? The cat or the mouse? I took a deep breath and tossed the bottle cap into the garbage where it plinked off the discarded bottle.

Turning, I started to make my way across the cracked and dirty linoleum when I saw him moving to meet me. I held the bottle out, placatory, praying silently. It did no good. He stepped forward, waiting for me at the end of the kitchen counter that separated the space from the living room, seemingly casual. He took the bottle from my outstretched hand and placed it carefully on the counter while, swift as a snake, his other hand reached out and grabbed my hair, yanking me towards him.

I stumbled and fell against him, defenseless from the curled right fist that came up swiftly to catch me just below my diaphragm. I felt every wisp of air as it was forcefully expelled. My diaphragm locked. Falling to my knees, I tried desperately to draw in breath, but my muscles were locked tight in a spasm. I fell to my side and spots began to dance. Then, whistling as loud as a hot tea kettle, a thin stream of air made it into my lungs. Slowly, I felt the muscles in my abdomen begin to relax and I drew in a lungful of air, the spots in my eyes receding.

He was still looming over me, watching dispassionately while I recovered. "What's for dinner?" He asked the question conversationally, as though nothing had happened.

I sat up, letting my hair fall around my face, a screening curtain, tears falling unheeded. I hunched over my knees for a moment, curling over my tender stomach, the pain now a dull ache. Suddenly, he grabbed my hair and yanked my head back, pulling me up viciously. I grabbed the counter edge to keep from hitting my head.

"I asked what's for dinner? You got hearin' problems, woman?"

"Beef and broccoli! Rice!" I gibbered, hands reaching for his, batting at them futilely. It felt like every hair in my head was being pulled out.

With a hard shove that sent me reeling back towards the refrigerator, he released his hold and turned away. I slumped against the side of the refrigerator, hands gently massaging my scalp where he'd pulled the hair, the skin tender beneath my questing fingers. I felt the trailer shake as he made his way down the hall.

My eyes roamed across the counter. The red and yellow label on the ant poison can gleamed brightly. I could hear him relieving himself, the sound echoing through the narrow confines of the structure.

I hated him so terribly. I began to shake, unable to still my trembling muscles, wracked with huge tremors. My eyes roamed from the cannister of ant poison to the withered buds of the broccolis in the colander, and beside them the pale gleam of the tiny mushrooms.

The mushrooms looked just like the ones they served at the Chinese all-you-could-eat buffet in the city. He always got a huge plate when we went. It had been a long time since we'd gone anywhere. A tear slid down my cheek as my heart suddenly seemed to pull in my chest, aching, throbbing. I had loved him so much! How could I have known that the tender and loving man I had met would become such a monster? He had been so handsome.

I saw him again as I had seen him on that warm May evening when we had first met. He had been tall, athletically built with a beautiful smile framing nice white teeth, a charming dimple creasing each corner of the kissable lips. I had fallen for him instantly. The courtship had been short, and marriage followed in a short span of time. Just as quickly, he began to reveal his true nature.

I looked around the dismal interior of the trailer. The dark wood paneling, the matted and clumped carpet stained into a strange pattern not dissimilar from tied-dye shirts, the original orangey-brown color only obvious in the protected areas under the end tables. Feeling the trailer shaking, I trekked his progress back into the living room, heard the protesting squeal as he sank back into the recliner, the metallic groan as the foot rest reluctantly rose to bear his weight.

I began to rinse the broccoli, pulling the sirloin out of the refrigerator. I set a pan of water on to boil and measured out the rice. Deftly I chopped the rubbery broccoli florets and then began to rinse the mushrooms.

They did look just like the ones at the restaurant. What did they call them? Oyster mushrooms, I thought, feeling that brief surge of brightness at recalling something so simple. Yes, they looked just like baby oyster mushrooms.

I was no expert on plants and had never gone mushroom hunting. There was no doubt at all in my mind, though, that the mushrooms in the bowl before me were deadly poison. I had found them growing in a small patch under the one large white oak at the edge of the dismal yard. The massive trunk offered a small area of perpetual shade and relative moisture for the fungus to take root. They may look like oyster mushrooms, but these were only a distant relative.

My hands trembling, I tumbled the bowl into the colander and began to rinse the dirt off the pallid white bits. I felt another tremor work through my muscles. One of excitement this time. I was going to do it! I was done being his whipping post. No more blows. No more hurtful comments. I smiled a little as I added the broccoli and mushrooms to the now simmering beef, pouring in a large quantity of soy sauce. The heavy salt flavor would mask anything unusual…wouldn't it?

I drifted into my thoughts as I watched the concoction simmer, stirring methodically, while my mind wandered. This would be a terrible way to go, I thought grimly. Then again, spending another ten or twenty or thirty years with him…and the immensity of all that time, all those dismal days to come…suddenly weighed terribly on my shoulders. It was more than a person could bear. The aroma of the beef and broccoli was actually quite good and my stomach gave a faint rumble.

I carefully fluffed the rice as I piled it in the center of the plate and then placed the beef mixture on top, noting as I did the small mushrooms that had darkened and shrunken after cooking, blending into the thick salty sauce. I made sure I had my portion as well.

I carried his plate in to him, using the television stand kept to one side and pulling it into place in front of him. My face flamed as he laid his hand across my right buttock, rubbing it.

"Think I'll get me some of that later," he grumbled as I slid the stand in front of him, stepping to the side and dislodging the sneaking hand.

I glanced at him, disgusted by the leer distorting his features. To appease him, I gave a faint smile and the very briefest of nods, hurrying back to the kitchen for my own plate.

As I resumed my seat in the corner of the couch, plate balanced on my lap, I watched him chew and swallow a bite, quickly followed by another forkful.

He glanced at me and grunted, waving the fork in my direction, a grain of sticky rice dropping to the floor unheeded. "Pretty good," he mumbled.

I smiled, and daintily took my first bite.

MOTHER'S TONGUE

Mom, this one is for you.

I am enchanted with the act of creation. At the first hint of spring, a glimpse of green peeking above a snow drift, and the need to get my hands in soil is a physical necessity. Nothing is more exciting than seeing your first seed sprout, and the joy of eating a tomato, still warm from the heat of an afternoon sun, that you grew from a tiny seed months ago when snow was still on the ground is, simply, incomparable in my opinion.

My chosen profession is also one of creation. I spin words for my living, creating worlds and people that seem to delight the fans that honor me with their readership. One of the first questions I am usually asked when I meet my fans is are your stories true? Now, if you are familiar with my writing, you'll know this question always gives me some pause. The women in my stories are strong and I don't mind being compared to them in that respect but that's about where the compliment ends. My characters usually have some significant warts. It is also an important consideration to realize that most of my stories don't have the traditional happy ending. Fortunately, in my case, real life does not imitate art.

I have a wonderful, supportive spouse. We are one of those lucky couples that still like each other after surpassing the decade milestone. In fact, we are approaching decade two and I am so grateful as I look back across the span of years and see few blemishes in the fabric. Oh, we aren't perfect, and we've had a time or two when things were touch and go. But that's the spice that makes a marriage flavorful with time. A good cook knows a little heat can perfect the dish.

But I digress. As I mentioned, most fans ask if my stories are based on real life and the answer is, no contest. Because there is no simple yes or no answer to that question. As any budding writer knows the first advice is to write about what you know. If you've never been in love, don't try to write a romance. It really is that simple. Write about what you know. So, yes, at times real life experiences may factor into my writing but a story is never based on real life. Except for this one. Something else a writer learns, and a basic fact of life, is that sometimes you just can't make it up. The greatest fiction is not as bizarre as real life.

It was a gorgeous Saturday morning in late April and the sun was shining brightly. For a change there was no wind, a gentle breeze blowing in off the lake. I'd cajoled my husband to helping me with the annual transplanting task. I have several very large plants that I divide every two years. While this is a job one person can manage, it's a job best handled by two.

We set up our work area on the back deck, me with six very large plants, and my husband with his reciprocal saw, fresh blade attached. We started on two Boston ferns and then moved on to two foxtail ferns. Motivated by this success, we proceeded on to the last two planned for that morning, two massive snake plants that I had picked up the previous fall at an estate sale. The plants had been crowding the planters and I fully expected the clay pots to crack before I could get them divided.

Now, I eyed the pots critically, taking the first and laying it its side on the large green garbage bag we were using as a drop cloth. I carefully levered the mass of stiff stems until I was able to fully remove the pot. Holding the plants upright, and carefully spreading the spiky leaves with my fingers, my husband cut through the clump with the saw and we quickly got the two plants resettled into new pots.

One more to go. We repeated the process and I held my breath as he guided the saw blade neatly into the middle of the clump. As I carefully pulled the two halves apart something gleamed in the dirt.

I called urgently to my husband, "Stop! Hold up a minute!"

He froze, working the blade back up and turning it off.

"What?" he asked, looking at me quizzically.

"There's something in here. Hold on a minute." My fingers closed around the object. I thought at first it was an old chain, perhaps part of a chainsaw. I pulled the chain carefully out of the tangle of roots that wove through it, dirt encrusting the links which shone a dull silver in the sun and laid it off to the side. Just a bit of gardening garbage that somehow made it into the pot when the plants were originally planted.

"Okay. You can go ahead now. Wouldn't have wanted that to foul up your blade."

He glanced at the bit of chain, nodded, and we finished splitting the plant. Twelve medium plants now proudly stood on the deck where there had been six. With an immense feeling of satisfaction, I turned my attention to the bit of chain, picking it up and running it through my fingers. As I did, I realized there was a clasp on one end. I stopped and peered a little closer at what lay in my hand.

The chain was the same length as the tennis bracelet my husband had gifted me on our fifth anniversary. My fingers brushed packed dirt and I saw that this was no chainsaw chain but an actual woman's bracelet. I looked at my husband and said, "Honey, look at this! I think it's a piece of jewelry!"

He had been rinsing his blade with water from the hose and I took the bracelet over to him, shoving it under the cold water. The encrusted dirt turned into mud and then began to rinse off, revealing a gleam from clear gems set in a metal that still had a bright sheen once the dirt was removed.

I gasped, turning the small section I had cleaned so the light caught and sparkled off the facets of the gems exposed. My eyes rose and locked with my husband's. "Good heavens! This looks valuable!"

I grasped the bracelet tightly and ran excitedly to the kitchen. A little effort with a soft brush under warm running water soon revealed a gleaming piece of jewelry which I carefully dried on a dish towel.

My husband came in and poured himself a cup of coffee, asking casually, "So, what've you got there?"

I spread the towel on the counter where the sun was shining through and carefully laid the bracelet out, waving my hand across it and inviting his inspection. "Take a look!"

I was understandably excited. Who knew how long the jewelry had been ensconced in the pot, nestled in amongst the tightly woven roots at the heart of the massive plant?

"Wow," my husband stated quietly, appreciating that this was no ordinary find.

I stroked a finger across the top. "This has to be a good metal. There's not a speck of rust anywhere. Look how shiny the metal is."

He nodded and asked, "What do you think the stones are?"

I raised my eyebrows and cocked my head on one side. "Hard to say. They look like diamonds…" I allowed the sentence to trail off. The stones were good sized, no mere chips. If these were indeed diamonds, this bracelet held a couple of karats easily. "I can't imagine setting a cheap stone in high quality metal, though."

This made him glance at me in surprise and then back at the bracelet with a new gleam in his eye. "What did you pay for those plants?" he asked.

I smiled. "Twenty bucks for the pair. Quite a deal, wouldn't you agree?"

I remembered the crisp fall day we'd attended the estate sale. We'd decided to take a drive to see fall foliage and we'd ended up in Branson, Missouri. Driving down a road that wound along beside Table Rock Lake we'd seen the sign for an estate sale. Well, there's not much we love more than rummaging around through yard sales, and estate sales are a special treat. This one had been no different except that it was the first day of the sale and we were there early. The seller had clearly been another plant lover and there had been several large plant specimens for sale, the two snake plants only a part of the impressive collection. These plants stood about four feet tall and were full to bursting in twenty-inch clay pots. I had always wanted a nice snake and here were two beautiful examples.

I turned pleading eyes on my husband.

He caught the glance and translated accurately, "What do you see?"

I ignored the slight tone of exasperation and gave him my brightest smile, hugging his arm close to my side, allowing just a subtle pressure against the side of my breast, "Well…" I drug the word out and turned my eyes back to the plants.

He followed my gaze and I felt him sort of slump in resignation while the deep sigh brushed hair tendrils on my temple. "Which ones?"

No question of his resignation remained but I cheerfully forged ahead. "Look at those two snake plants, honey. Aren't they amazing? Those poor babies need transplanting so bad…"

"And let me guess, you just feel the need to take them home, and baby them, and nurture them."

"Exactly! See how well you know me?" I squeezed his arm again.

"I don't know, babe. Those plants are pretty big. I'm not sure they'll fit in the truck."

"Don't be silly! Of course, they'll fit. We can raise the back seat, they'll fit easily." And they had. I'd wintered them over in our master bedroom where they got nice filtered southern light.

"What do you think it's worth?" my husband asked, breaking into my reverie and bringing me back to the present.

"I couldn't begin to guess. I suppose I could take it and get it appraised."

Which is what I ended up doing. One of my favorite television shows to watch is *Antique Roadshow*. I've always fantasized what it would be like to discover that old Great-Aunt Marie's vase that everyone thought was so horrendously ugly was worth five figures. Not that I have a Great-Aunt Marie or her ugly vase, but you know what I mean. Wouldn't we all like to discover we have something that's worth a lot of money? Well, I got to find out what that's like that day at the jewelers.

As we sat down to eat that evening, my husband busily cutting into the chili cheese dogs that I learned early in our marriage were a dietary staple that he required no less than once monthly, I casually dropped the bracelet onto the placemat next to his plate.

He masticated his mouthful of hot dog and, chasing it with soda, asked, "Got it appraised?" before proceeding with the next forkful.

I nodded and replied, "Yep. Care to take a guess?"

He eyed the bracelet, pushing it around with his finger before asking, "They say how many karats?"

I smiled and nodded. "Four."

"Four!" His hand jerked back as if the bracelet were hot before tentatively touching it again and repeating softly, "Four."

My smile grew broader and I had to hide the slight trembling in my hand by putting it in my lap to fiddle with my napkin.

"Hmm." He took another bite and chewed thoughtfully. "Fifteen hundred," he ventured.

"More." I said softly.

"What? How much, babe?"

"Almost eight grand."

He had been taking a drink of soda and he spluttered, splashing me and his plate with a small fountain. My timing has always been bad.

"Oh, goodness!" I exclaimed, dashing to get a towel to mop up the worst of it.

"Did you say eight thousand?" His voice sounded strained.

I checked quickly to make sure he wasn't choking, requiring me to call on never used first aid knowledge, but saw that he was just in a mild state of shock. Food forgotten he was holding the bracelet in his hands, looking closely at the gleaming diamonds.

I resumed my seat and told him, "According to the jeweler, those are VS1-VS2 quality diamonds. There are fifty-three total in what's called a round cut. They are graded an F, which means they are third class...a very good quality of stone. The setting is platinum."

The silence drug out as he stared into my eyes. "Honey, this is amazing," he finally said.

I smiled a little wistfully and held my hand out.

He shook his head. "No," he said, "Let me put it on you."

I hesitated, hand reaching, and then allowed him to clasp the bracelet around my wrist. It fit perfectly and the dance of light across the facets was hypnotizing. I turned my wrist, watching the colors flash. Then I shook my head and carefully took it off, laying it on the table before us.

"I have to do the right thing," I finally said.

"Which is?" he asked, his tone a shade belligerent, no doubt anticipating my next words.

"I have to take it back, of course."

He sat back and snorted. "Back? Back where?"

I laid my fork beside my plate and sat back. "I'd love to keep it, but I'd be scared of wearing it. I doubt we'd ever get what the jeweler says it's worth, but I know we could get something. Trust me, I've been through this in my mind a thousand times today." I looked at him pleadingly, "But this bracelet meant something to someone. It doesn't feel right to just keep it."

He studied my face solemnly for a moment, and then he smiled, his face softening. "There's the woman I love." He leaned across and I met him halfway, our lips tenderly caressing.

I sat back, warmth infusing me, appreciating again the amazing love I felt for this man.

He picked up his fork and knife and again attacked his now slightly soggy chili cheese dog, asking, "So, what's the first step?"

Delivering on my intent ended up being considerably more difficult than I had at first thought it would be. The first hurdle was locating the house where the estate sale had been. We piled into the truck the following Saturday morning and headed for Branson. I was confident I knew where the house was. Until we'd gone down four roads that wound along the lake and each, I swore, was the right road. Only I never did spot the house my memory vaguely recalled. Naturally it would look different. There would, for one thing, not be a handy sign. Nor would there more be the overabundance of vehicles in the drive or along the road as there had been that day. Still, I thought to myself irritably, I should recognize it.

Winding our way back to the main road, I slumped disconsolately in the passenger seat.

"Let's get some lunch and we'll try again." My husband said cheerfully, pulling over and fiddling with the map program on his cell phone. "What are you hungry for?"

I shrugged. "Not really hungry," I mumbled.

"Oh, come on! Worst case you get a nice bracelet for twenty bucks. *And* two plants. Don't forget the plants."

"Nice!" I exclaimed, outraged.

He shrugged and laughed, signaling to pull back onto the road, eyes on his side mirror. "Okay. Maybe a bit more than nice."

I sighed heavily and gazed out the window at the passing scenery, homes nestled snuggly amongst the towering trees. "It just isn't right," I finally said. "I just *know* that bracelet means a lot to someone. She wouldn't have parted with it, I'm certain."

My husband smiled tolerantly and said, "We'll find it, sweetheart. How does fried chicken sound? The best in Branson...or so the ratings claim."

He was correct, as he usually is. The fried chicken was the best I'd had in a restaurant in some time, and we both agreed we'd found a place we'd like to come back to in the future.

He was also correct about finding the house. The first road we turned down after leaving the restaurant seemed vaguely familiar, but so had the other ones. It was when we came around a turn, the lake appearing on our left, and I saw the house perched above the road that it clicked that *this* was the house. "Stop!" I cried out, pointing excitedly. "This is it!"

We pulled up the paved curving drive and parked in front of the detached two car garage, my heart sinking as he put the truck in park. The house was all too obviously vacant. Weeds were springing up riotously around the formerly neat beds that accentuated the front of the house and there was an air of gloomy neglect just settling over the handsome structure. Black and blind windows gazed vacantly out towards the sparkling blue waters of the lake, power boats seemingly flying across the slightly choppy surface, the drone of their motors a constant thrum under the cacophony of bird song.

"There's no one here," I said, crushed with disappointment.

"Well, let's just have a look around," following words with actions as he exited the truck, walking purposefully towards the front door.

I waited in the truck, knowing no one would come to his knock, hopefully watching all the same. He waited patiently and tried knocking one more time. After another brief pause, he stepped over to the large bay window that fronted the house to the right of the door. Cupping his hands, he peered into the room beyond. He didn't stay long, shoving his hands in his jacket pockets and heading back to the truck.

"Empty," he announced, sliding behind the wheel. "There's a realtors sign leaning on the wall in the front room."

"Oh?" I asked. This might be the lead I needed.

He executed a turn in the area provided and headed back out to the road. "Home?" he asked.

"Sure. So, could you see which realtor?"

"Yeah."

Silence.

He could be so exasperating, and he loved to pull my chain at any chance. "Do you have plans on sharing?" I asked a little tartly.

"Share what?" He was all innocence.

I rolled my eyes. "The realtor! What's the name?"

He smiled, "It looked like it said Sunset Realty. Bet you can find them on the internet."

I pulled a pen and found a crumpled wad of receipt to use as paper and scribbled down the name. "Thank you." If my tone was a little prim, well, he deserved it.

The next evening, as we sat down to breakfast for dinner, a favorite in our house, I proudly announced, "I think I know her name."

My husband grinned appreciatively at his plate of French toast and began to liberally drown it in syrup. "Oh?" he inquired politely.

"Mmm hmm," I said, taking a bite of my grilled chicken and apple smoked sausage. There was silence as we both savored our meal.

Finally, he asked, "So? Do you plan on telling me?"

"Consuela Paramus."

"That's a mouthful!"

I shot him a disapproving look. "It's a beautiful name. It just rolls right off your tongue." And I said it again, slowly, savoring the play of vowels and consonants. "Consuela Paramus." I sighed. "It sounds so romantic, doesn't it?"

He merely grunted in response.

"She was married to Jackson. Jackson Paramus." I took another bite of dinner and then added, "Consuela and Jackson Paramus. I wonder if he went by Jack or Jackson? Connie and Jack? Or Consuela and Jackson?"

Not even a grunt now.

"I think I prefer Consuela and Jackson."

"So, what happened to them?"

The internet is a wonderful thing and with the little the realtor had been able to provide me, which wasn't much more than Consuela's name, I had been able to piece together a skeleton of their backstory based on public records. "Consuela and Jackson bought the property where the house is in early 2003. The house was built in 2004, so they must have started right away. They've lived there ever since. Jackson passed away in 2012. June of 2012."

"Too bad," my husband offered commiseratively, and I studied him closely, feeling that special warmth when I felt his honest compassion. He can be such a tender man.

"Yes," I agreed. "That's about all I know. The realtor said he thought Mrs. Paramus had sold the house and moved to New Mexico to be near her daughter but he wasn't certain, and he didn't know the daughter's name. He said a local auction company handled the estate sale."

My husband was quiet for a moment, absorbing this, before saying, "Well, honey, at least you tried."

"Tried?" I was immediately on alert. "This isn't over by any means. That's just all I was able to find out *today*. I've got to set it aside for a few days…that deadline on the short story collection is coming up and I'm still short one story." A tiny light bulb went on as an idea was hatched.

It was a week later that I dropped the next bombshell on my darling of a husband. We were eating dinner, which seems to be the hour I strike, and he had just finished telling me about his day when he chose the wrong selection of words. "So, tell me about your day."

That is such an innocuous little statement. If only he had asked *How was your day?* That could be easily answered with a simple *Great!* or *Wonderful!* Pick the adjective of your choice. But, *tell me about your day* was an entirely different question.

"Well," I began slowly, "I was able to get back to my research on Consuela."

"That a character in your new story?" he asked in seeming innocence.

Exasperated, I shook my head. "No. Not my new story. Not a character. Does a diamond bracelet ring any bells, darling?"

He shot me a look that said he did not appreciate my use of sarcasm and merely said, "Oh."

I felt contrite immediately. I smiled brightly and forged on. "It took a bit of digging but I found the daughter. She'd gotten married, so, of course, her last name wasn't Paramus. I went back through some old Branson news archives and found a story about one Rebecca Paramus, the daughter of Consuela and Jackson Paramus, was to marry a Kevin Crumpler on such and such a date, yada yada. The couple planned to make their new home in Deming, New Mexico."

"Wow. Good job," my husband said, admiration in his tone.

I nodded and smiled, "Thank you. It was easy work from there to locate an address for the Crumpler's through the New Mexico public records for property taxes. It took a bit, but I had Deming as a possible and searched Luna County first. There they were!"

"Impressive! Now what? Did you call them?"

Here came the big moment and I took a deep breath. "No. I don't think this is the sort of thing you can do over the phone." I hesitated and kept my eyes on my plate, which didn't prevent me from feeling his drilling into me.

"A letter?" he asked softly, adding even more hopefully, "An email? Send a pic? That's a great idea!" he finished gamely.

I looked at him and tried to look my most pleading, sad eyes and all, "A little trip, honey. And it would be a tax write off!" I added brightly.

He got a suspicious look on his face, the look I thought of as his *Lucy, what have you done* look.

"No, really," I said seriously. "I plan on writing about this. In fact, I've already started." I sat back and crossed my arms, ready to go to battle on this if need be. "I priced the air fare. We could fly into El Paso on Southwest, rent a car, stay one night…and we still wouldn't be out five hundred dollars."

He raised an eyebrow in disbelief, and I shrugged. "Okay, maybe a little bit more but not much. Besides, it would be nice to have a long weekend and a short vacation."

"When?" His tone was challenging.

I shrugged. "I don't know. Maybe in six weeks?".

He raised his eyebrows again. "New Mexico in mid-June?"

"Sure!" I'd done my research and was ready. "If we're lucky the poppies will be blooming." In actuality I knew this was pretty unlikely, but it had seemed like a nice selling point. We'd be several months too late, and New Mexico had had a moderately dry winter, the wrong conditions entirely.

"Poppies?" Clearly, he wasn't all that impressed by the selling point.

"It's a nice time to visit, really. The temps are in the eighties, maybe nineties, during the day and downright cold at night. Deming is in the high dessert." I announced this smugly, proud of my new-found knowledge. Secretly, I actually was looking forward to visiting this otherwise unheard-of place. The little I'd seen online was intriguing.

Deming did not disappoint. At first, as my husband pulled the compact rental car onto west bound Interstate Ten, I was dismayed by the landscape. The homes on the Mexico side of the border are clustered closely together, jutting out above steep ravines. Interstate Ten runs very close to the border here. Then the road begins to wind away, and you sense you are gaining altitude. Tall, sandy colored peaks thrust jaggedly up into the cobalt blue sky.

I wish I could say Deming is beautiful. To me, it is not. It is stark and surrounded by desert. There are groves of pecans and large fields with solar panel arrays. The mountains, however, are stunning. The Crumpler's adobe ranch-style home sat facing the Florida mountains to the east. And that is *not* pronounced like Florida the state. The *i* is pronounced like a long *e*. It's a dead giveaway that you're an out of towner if you pronounce it like Florida the state.

I strode through the harsh, late June sun, marveling once again at a dust twister racing across a field in the far distance, and pressed the doorbell button, hearing the distant sound of the chimes. I nervously twisted my hands and smiled broadly when a woman opened the inner door and peered out the intervening storm door at me, her hand on the latch.

I smiled as reassuringly as I could and asked, "Are you Rebecca Crumpler?"

She cocked her head a little to one side and nodded briefly, opening the door and edging out to stand beside me on the small front deck area, decorated nicely with succulents in colorful pots. "I'm Becky Crumpler."

She was probably in her mid-fifties with brown hair and brown eyes, skin tanned a golden color. She wore her hair in a short, tight cap of curls. I held out my hand and said, "I'm Christine Wade. Please, call me Chris. I'm actually looking for your mother. Consuela." I paused hopefully.

She looked at me in surprise and interest, a small frown creasing her forehead. "Why are you interested in my mother?"

I took a deep breath. "It's a long story, Becky, but I found something very valuable that I believe belongs to your mother. I would like to return it to her."

Becky studied me pensively for a moment, her eyes wandering to the dark blue rental car where my husband Lewis sat baking in the triple digit temperature. So much for eighties or nineties. She looked back at me inquiringly and I explained, "That's my husband. He came with me. We're from Arkansas."

"Wow! That's a long way to come to return something." Her eyes searched mine and then she nodded. "Okay. My mom lives in town. She's at Mariposa Village. Here, I'll write it down for you, if you'll wait a moment?"

"I'd be very grateful. Yes, thank you."

Becky disappeared into the house and returned a short time later with a piece of paper that she held out to me. "I'll call Mom and tell her you're on the way over."

She flapped her hand at me when I glanced at her in alarm and continued quickly, "I'm not going to tell her *why* you're here, just that someone wants to visit. So she won't be surprised, and has a minute to straighten up."

I considered that and volunteered, "You know, there are a few things I need to pick up. I could do a little shopping. Maybe the hotel would let us check in early. I could, maybe, plan to be at your mom's in about two hours?"

Becky smiled broadly and said, "Perfect." She held her hand out and we shook firmly, and she said, "A pleasure meeting you. Safe travels back to Arkansas."

It actually took two hours and fifteen minutes before we appeared on Consuela's doorstep. Checking into the hotel had taken a bit more time than anticipated when there was a thirty-minute delay for housekeeping to verify the room was ready. Lewis insisted we wait since we were already here anyway and wandered to the bar area to have a cold beer and watch the baseball game on television.

Consuela was obviously prepared for company. A cut crystal pitcher filled with what could only be homemade lemonade sat on a silver tray on the dark wood of the coffee table, glasses with ice waiting. A tray with assorted cookies, a stack of small plates and pile of napkins stood invitingly beside the drinks.

Consuela herself was a beautiful, diminutive woman. Soaking wet she might have weighed a hundred, but I doubted it. Her hair was still naturally dark along her back hairline, iron gray over the top and worn in a braid that hung to the middle of her slightly stooped back. She was dressed attractively in a white linen loose top and pants, tan knit loafers on her feet. A strand of pink pearls hung at her neck, matching posts in her ears.

She settled into a wingback chair, back to the window, facing across the table from us, Lewis and I sitting together on a love seat. She gracefully poured us each a glass of lemonade and waved elegantly at the cookies, "Help yourselves." Her voice was a deep, surprising alto, soft and warm.

"Thank you," I said, sipping at the lemonade. "Oh! This is quite good!" I was pleasantly surprised.

Consuela smiled. "A secret recipe. I make a simple syrup and add a fresh sprig of thyme while it cooks. I strain the thyme out after I let it steep in the lemonade for a bit."

"You don't mind if I write that down quick, do you?" I asked, pulling a small pad from my purse and ignoring Lewis' barely audible groan. I discreetly nudged him with my elbow.

Consuela smiled, "Not at all." She waited patiently while I scribbled down some quick notes on the lemonade before asking, "So, what brings you all the way from Arkansas?"

I set the glass down on the coaster provided and asked, "Did you sell a house on Table Rock Lake near Branson last October and did you have an estate sale there just before?"

Consuela nodded and said, "Why, yes, I did."

I nodded. "I went to that estate sale and I purchased two large snake plants. Do you by any chance recall them?"

Her smile grew tender and her eyes seemed to look off into the far distance. "Yes," she said softly, "I remember those plants. We didn't call them snake plants, of course. They're known as Mother's Tongue in the South." She smiled and sipped her tea. "They were in dreadful need of transplanting." She was silent for a moment, her eyes focused on the past. Finally, she stirred, her eyes catching mine. "So, you bought them? I hope you split them."

I chuckled. "Oh, yes. First thing this spring."

She nodded happily. "I had those plants for years. At one time I had twelve of them!" Her eyes were round with delight, once again seeing her past, not the present. "It was a semi-annual tradition. My husband would help me. We'd split the plants. But then he passed…" Her voice trailed off and her face became incredibly sad. I felt my heart pull in my chest. "It became too much for me." She looked directly at me again and I could see her pain.

I swallowed and struggled to speak. Before I could, she continued.

"I gave ten plants away after he passed. I kept those last two. I always planned to split them, but it was just too much for me to do alone. I was afraid I'd shatter the pots, kill the plants." She shook her head. "I didn't want that to happen, so I just kept them alive. Finally had to let them go in the estate sale. Couldn't move them here."

I had managed to swallow the lump in my throat. "Mrs. Paramus, did you ever lose a piece of jewelry?"

She looked at me quizzically, frowning. "Let me think." Her eyes once again drifted away and into the past and I saw the first stir of memory as she said, "Why yes…" Her eyes flew back to mine, searching eagerly. "Oh, my heavens, is it possible…?" she breathed.

I nodded and pulled the slim jeweler's box out of my purse, holding it across the table. She extended shaking hands and I saw the first splash of a tear on the back of her hand. She cracked open the case and gazed at the diamond bracelet nestled on a bed of black velvet, stones gleaming. I heard a rasping gasp and a deep moaning sob escape her before she raised her hand and cried openly. She laid the case in her lap and her other hand groped for a box of tissues that stood on the table beside her. I rose quickly and guided the box to her hand.

I settled back on the couch next to Lewis, politely looking away from Consuela, patting his leg and listening as he chewed on a cookie. Slowly, Consuela's breathing returned to normal, she dabbed carefully at her eyes and placed the soggy tissue in a wad in her lap, lifting the bracelet to gaze at it in wonder. "All this time I wondered where it was, where it had gone. It was a gift from my dear husband on our fiftieth wedding anniversary. Wherever did you find it?"

I laughed. "It was all snarled up in the roots of the Mother's Tongue. When we split it, there it was," I shrugged.

"My dear child," she said in wonder. "And you came all this way to return it? Have you any idea it's value?"

I nodded, smiling happily. "It wasn't the value that was important. I just knew that this had to be special to you."

"You have no idea," she said, grasping the case tightly. "I can remember the day we met like it was only yesterday. I was leaving church with my friend. He told me later, that when he saw me, he told his friend, *There's the girl I'm gonna' marry.*" She looked at me and I saw a mischievous twinkle in her eyes. "That was in Massachusetts. That's where I lived, and he was in the Air Force. Oh, he was a handsome man!"

Lewis coughed politely and she chuckled, "You were very correct, Christine. This bracelet means an awful lot to me and I am so very grateful that you have returned it. My husband and I were blessed to share fifty-six wonderful years together." Again, she got a mischievous look and chuckled. "There are fifty-three stones. When Jackson gave it to me on our fiftieth, he joked that he only had to endure three more. A stone for every year." Her voice caught on another half sob, a slight hitch, before she continued, "I was fortunate to get three more."

Returning that bracelet to Consuela was an incredibly rewarding experience and I have made a friend for life in Deming, New Mexico. We had a very enjoyable visit and it turns out there's actually quite a lot to do in the area. If the scenery is not exactly to my taste it is starkly beautiful in its very own unique and special way and the people are wonderful.

My husband enjoyed the experience as well and was just showing me some discount airfare to El Paso that we could get a deal on. When I'd reached for his hand, he'd grabbed mine, planting a kiss on my palm and turning my wrist to admire the flash.

"I still can't believe she gave it to you," he said wonderingly.

I studied the fifty-three round cut diamonds set in platinum shining improbably on my wrist as we ate Sloppy Joes and I smiled. "We just celebrated eighteen. Only thirty-five more to go!" before leaning over and kissing him passionately, dinner forgotten.

RICOCHET

We were only fourteen and it was the dog days of August, when you feel sticky from dried perspiration on hot skin, the air is dry and unsatisfying when you inhale, the act of thinking is exhausting. Yet our young bodies thrummed with excitement as we gazed at what Trent held in the palm of his hand.

The sounds of the slums, the never-ending whine of sirens...near and far...the screaming infants sweltering in the heat with no relief in airless cribs surrounded by protective layers of wafted cotton, stifling any chance breeze; all had faded into a distant drone in the background. We were so used to it, it was so ingrained, it was not something we noticed.

Mothers leaned out of windows high above us and shouted into the general mayhem where their offspring spent most of their days, ordering them to do whatever current task was at hand. We didn't hear them either. Somehow, though, we always heard our own mother's. Another skill acquired out of necessity.

The gun looked heavy. I'd seen lots of them before, of course, but always out of reach. Always flashed around by the bigger, older boys. Trent hefted it. The black steel gleamed in the hot sunlight, dazzling, everything else dusty and drab in comparison.

"Is it loaded?" I asked in a bare whisper, awe silencing my voice. My right hand hanging at my side twitched and jerked involuntarily, wanting to touch it...the steel looking like it would feel like a block of ice on this triple digit day.

"Wouldn't be much good now if it wasn't, would it?" Trent seemed to have acquired an authority he didn't have before. He didn't look any different, but he sounded different. We'd been best friends since we started grade school together.

"Lemme hold it."

Trent hesitated; I could see his reluctance to hand it over. I remembered watching that movie with all those funny characters in it…elves and weird looking monsters…and this little scrawny dude…I remember his name was Golump or something like that. Anyway, there was this ring that was magical, and this creature had it and lost it and went nuts trying to find it. Well, that's what Trent sort of reminded me of for about ten or twenty seconds. Then, slowly, he held it out to me.

"Man, you got to be careful."

"I got this. I ain't stupid." I knew the business part, knew where not to put my fingers and to keep the barrel away from Trent or myself. And it was heavy. Surprisingly heavy. When Trent laid it on my open palm, I wasn't expecting the weight.

"Watch it!" Trent called out in alarm.

I grabbed a tighter hold on the gun and laughed nervously.

Trent laughed, too. "I told you it was heavy."

We both admired it in my hand. I felt something like electricity in my muscles. Wires were going helter-skelter in my nervous system, doing a dance along my skin, and I felt my scalp tingle. I'd never felt anything like it and suddenly couldn't get enough of it. "Where'd you get it?"

"Nah, I can't tell you that."

"Since when do we keep secrets?"

"Since now."

I didn't have much to say to that. I handed the gun back.

The big bass boom of a low rider cruising down the block filled the air with vibrations and Trent shoved the gun in his waistband and pulled his shirt over. We stood there trying to look casual while we watched a rigged out, black and chrome, badass Dodge Charger cruise by, five guys crammed in, two in front and three in back. They looked us over real hard as they drove by but decided we weren't worth messing with. They passed and turned the next corner, the bass carrying back to us until it got swallowed by the general mayhem of the city.

The gun reappeared in Trent's hand.

"Whatcha' gonna do with it?" I asked.

Trent hitched his left shoulder in a half shrug. "Dunno. I jes' like havin' it."

That seemed reasonable enough to me. We just stood in silence for a bit looking at it some more. Trent turning it over, showing me how it worked…dropping the clip from the butt stock, taking the safety on and off.

Trent took the gun home shortly after that when his mom hollered at him to come and help her. I quickly grew bored and headed in to play some video games.

We started back to school the following week. It was a big change for us. We'd moved up to the ninth grade and were entering high school as freshmen. It was not something either one of us was looking forward to.

Eighth grade had seemed like a reprieve, of sorts. We were the oldest kids in school, if anyone did any pushing it was liable to be one of us. Trent and I both had gotten our share of being pushed around though Trent had it worse than I did. I'm not sure if it was his slightly different look…he had fair skin that turned red easily and was apt to do so when he got upset along with light brown hair that had just a touch of red in sunlight. His eyes were a muddy brown and looked red at times, too. He was short and real thin, very wiry. I had about fifteen pounds on him and he could still beat me at wrestling. Not all the time, we were pretty evenly matched and if I got a good hold on him it was all over. But he was hell to hold, slippery as an eel. He'd beaten lots bigger kids in gym class when we had wrestling matches. I don't guess that helped much with his popularity. Who wants to be beaten by the short runty kid?

Trent was smart, too. He didn't show it off, didn't hang with the other smart kids. They didn't like him much, either, it seemed. He'd created a tough demeanor for himself. Tough isn't really the right word. There're cliques in school. A jock group, a smart group, a tough group. Funny how kids strive to fit stereotypes. I see that now as I look back. We tried so hard to discover our own individuality, while working even harder to fill the stereotype of who we thought we were or wanted to be.

Trent didn't fit any of those stereotypes. I think that's what made him different. He was an individual while the rest of the herd around him hadn't figured that out yet. Trent wasn't one of the tough ones. He didn't smoke cigarettes in the bathroom with the other toughies who scattered like cockroaches when a teacher appeared through the smoke haze.

No, he was tough with words. He was the wise ass of the class. They might make fun of him, but he could make them laugh. He was every teacher's nemesis. The smart kid with the sarcastic mouth and dry wit. When he succeeded in making the class laugh, I think in his eyes, for just a minute, they liked him. And for just that minute they did like him. And they envied that easy wit. Trent exuded a grace that was not natural for his age.

Returning now to high school as freshmen turned everything upside down. We'd be back under the pressures of the same kids we'd struggled against since elementary school. Sixth grade wasn't that long ago, and it was easy to remember the teasing and intimidation of the then eighth graders. Only now there would be yet another grade to torment the younger kids, the seniors. We all knew the stakes were higher in high school, the game rougher.

The sophomores were the worst. They'd been the freshmen just the previous year and they carried their grudges in the form of payback to the fresh crop. Seniors and juniors were known to torment both sophomores and freshmen…but only the disliked sophomores. Any freshman was fair game. Most seniors didn't pay the younger grades any mind at all, and it was the same with most juniors. Their thoughts and actions reflected a step towards an uncertain future, little time to consider time recently past.

There were several sophomores that Trent and I would both prefer to avoid. The first week of new classes was spent scoping out their proximity as much as getting adjusted to the new and much larger school and far more complicated daily schedule we had to keep up with.

Trent and I didn't share that many classes. We had English, History and Phys Ed together. Our lunch schedule was the same, too. We had the earlier lunch at 11:30. Not all our classes were located near one another and it was often a mad dash to get to the next class before the bell rang. It was during these dashes down halls that we kept a watch for any of our foes. We spotted some early the first week, mostly just passing in halls, but two of them were in our Phys Ed class. That was pretty bad. Worst, a whole gang of them shared our lunch period.

It was our third week back and we had worked out an arrangement to meet at the south entrance to the cafeteria. There was a small lobby with bench seating along the wall and a bank of lockers across from the entrance to the cafeteria. It was usually a busy place and today was no different. My last class before lunch was Spanish, and my room was pretty close, so it was usually me that waited on Trent, who had to come all the way from the far west wing where he had Algebra. Today my Spanish teacher, Mr. Collins, had kept us right up to the bell and a few minutes late giving us our homework assignments. As I approached the south entrance to the cafeteria, I felt the tension that always exists when a crowd of people are watching a fight. I felt my stomach sink when I saw Trent in the middle of the gang of sophomores that liked to bully him, a large crowd jostling around them.

I heard the largest of the group say, "Come on, Shrimp. Hand over your lunch money. I done told you…my dad gave mine to your mom, as payment for the blow job she give him."

The other four flanking him, encircling Trent, giggled.

A red flush crept up Trent's cheeks. He kept his eyes on his toes, not looking up at the menacing group surrounding him. I saw him shift his weight, a slight rocking motion heel to toe, just barely perceptible. Then, he shocked me, raising his head and staring Keith, the bully running his mouth, straight back and saying, "Yeah, well, my mom said it was that cheap cause your dads got such a tiny dick."

For a second, I think my heart stuttered. I know that lobby went dead silent and every kid that could hear held his breath. Trent's cheeks were still flushed but it was an angry hectic red now, his neck splotched. I shot a quick glance at Keith to gauge his reaction.

He seemed to be equally stunned. For a minute he just stood and stared at Trent, assessing him. Then he threw his head back and laughed. "Good one, kid! Damn, I think you're learning!" He gave Trent a weak punch on his shoulder, still laughing, almost chummy now. "I'll give you that one, that was pretty good." He wiped the back of his hand across his mouth and then put his hand on the shoulder of the kid next to him. "Come on. Let's go get some grub."

The group dissolved and dispersed into the noisy cafeteria. I stood and stared for a moment longer at Trent. Here was another example of the change I'd seen in him since he'd found the gun. He never would have stood up to Keith before. He took a deep breath, collecting himself and the flush receded from his face and neck. He glanced around and saw me across the lobby.

I tried to act like I'd just walked up and sent him a quick if shaky smile. "Hey! Mr. Collins was a real jerk and kept us after the bell."

"That sucks," he responded shortly.

"Yeah." I waited to see if he'd say more but he just turned and headed for the cafeteria. I stood for a second, watching his stiff back as he strode away. There would be repercussions from Keith. Keith wasn't likely to let this go as he'd implied. He'd just been caught by surprise. I figured Trent had to know that, too.

I noticed other changes in Trent as fall changed to winter and we broke for Thanksgiving. Where he'd once been bright and full of ideas, always joshing about a way to pull a prank on someone...both of us knowing he'd never follow through but enjoying the fantasies he created...he instead became withdrawn and sullen. We weren't hanging out together as much after school, either.

Walking home one afternoon, I brought it up, "Hey, you never hang out anymore. Whatcha' got goin' on?"

He gave a half shrug, hunching his head into the shoulder nearest me and shifted his books from his left hand to his right hand. "Nothin'. Mom's been working evenings at the diner and I've got to watch Erin."

"Oh."

We walked a bit further in awkward silence, a tension I was unaccustomed to between us. I wanted to make it go away, wanted things to be the way they'd been. "You still got it?" I finally asked.

"Hunh?" He glanced at me, frowning. "Got what?"

"You know!" I whispered. "The gun!"

"Shhh!" Trent instantly hushed me and looked around furtively even though there was no one anywhere near us. "'Course."

"Oh." I didn't know what else to say. We walked along as another awkward silence settled over us. I felt relief as we turned onto our street and I could see the tenement up ahead. "So, anyway, I've got a new game for my PlayStation. Well, it's not new. I got it down at The Game Shop...used, but so what? It's X-Men: Mutant Academy. You should come over. Check it out."

Trent showed some real interest, a spark in his eyes. I knew he loved X-Men. Just then, as he was looking at me, he stumbled and the stack of books and papers in his right hand went flying.

"Shit!" He yelled and made a futile grab for the scattering pages.

I dropped my own pile on the pavement and dove after the nearest errant stack before they could blow into the street. As I scooped them up my eyes caught the headlines on the printed pages: Umpqua Community College Shooting; Parkland, Florida High School Shooting; Another Deadly High School Shooting: This Time in Santa Fe, Texas. I looked up from the pages to meet Trent's steady gaze. He held his hand out for the pages and I thrust them at him. "What's that all about?" I asked, curious.

"Project for Social Studies. Doing a paper on violence in school's today."

"Oh." I nodded, and we continued home.

The next day in sixth period Biology, I sat beside Jude, a friend Trent and I hung out with quite a bit. I knew he was in Social Studies with Trent and so I asked him about the project they were working on.

"What project?" He asked, puzzled.

"I don't know," I replied. "Something about violence in schools?"

Jude slouched back in his seat, frowning. "Don't know what you're talkin' about. We're reading some shit about post-Civil War government in the South. Like who gives two shits about that today."

"Oh." I was confused. Why had Trent lied to me, and if he didn't have those print outs for Social Studies, then why did he have them?

The following week was the start of winter break and we'd be out for two weeks. I knew I'd be spending some time with Trent; he'd said he was going to come over that Saturday to play X-Men, and maybe I'd find out what was really going on with him.

Instead, when I got home that Friday evening my mom excitedly announced, "Go pack some things quick! I've got a week off and we're going to visit your Aunt Melinda!" She was rushing around the kitchen, throwing snacks and canned sodas into a cooler sitting open in the middle of the kitchen floor.

"Trent was gonna come over tomorrow…" I started, lamely realizing how very unimportant this announcement was.

She paused and gave me that look that asked how could I possibly be her offspring, resting her hands on her hips as she slowly shook her head. "Well, really. And you saw him…what? All of maybe two minutes ago? Run over and let him know there's been a change in plans. You can see him when you get back." Having delivered this pronouncement from on high with the absolute authority of an adult she went back to sorting through the open refrigerator.

I went and did as instructed but ended up not seeing Trent when we got back from my Aunt's. His little sister Erin had been down sick and was just recovering. His mom didn't want any risk of any germs getting her sick again. I thought maybe he'd come visit me, but he said his mom didn't want him bringing anything home and who knew what I might have been exposed to.

The two weeks of winter break was just long enough for us to forget about the incident with Keith. I should have known that was exactly what Keith had been waiting for. We had Phys Ed third period every Tuesday and Thursday. Coach had us running basketball drills so when you got changed into your uniform you were to come out of the locker and start running dribbles along the court line until he blew the whistle to gather into formation. Trent had been struggling with the lace on his right shoe and I'd run out, leaving him behind. Coach was busy talking to the second Coach, who was running drills with tenth graders on the other half of the court, divided now with the artificial wall they used to split the court so two gym classes could be held at the same time. There was a plan to open the court and have a match between the two grades in early February.

I dribbled for what seemed like a long time before Coach Smith blew the whistle and we fell into a disorderly row across the court. Coach pulled out his clipboard and began to call out our names. I looked around for Trent but didn't see him.

Eventually Coach got to Trent's name and there was no response. He looked around, made a mark on his clipboard and called the next name. My heart sank when neither Cody or Ronnie responded, either. They were Keith's two cronies. I suddenly had a bad feeling in my stomach. Coach finished going through the list and looked around again. "Anyone know where Trent, Cody or Ronnie might be?"

I opened my mouth to speak but found it was spit dry…my tongue was not able to move. A croak of some sort escaped, and I closed my mouth, gulping quickly in an effort to produce saliva. Finally, I felt my vocal chords unlock. "Locker!" I managed to squeak.

"What?" Coach craned his head towards me. "What was that Robertson?"

I cleared my throat. "I saw Trent in the locker room. I know he's here, sir."

Coach frowned and tucked his clipboard under his arm. "Well, please do us the kindness to go ask Mr. Trent Brown to pleasure us with his presence, if you would be so kind?"

His smile was anything but a match to the syrupy tone of his voice.

"Sure." I turned and jogged back to the locker room entrance. Before I could get there Cody and Ronnie came out, queer looks on their faces. I stopped to let them pass and was turning to enter the locker when I heard Keith's voice echoing off the cinderblock walls.

"Won't be such a smart-ass next time, will you?" I heard the click of heels on cement and Keith strode out of the locker room, a snicker on his face. For a second our eyes met, and he laughed in a low and mean way before turning and leaving the court while Cody and Ronnie sauntered over to the line.

I turned and rushed into the locker room. Trent was kneeling next to the first row of benches as you come out of the shower. His face was streaked with tears, his lips were bruised and already swelling, blood trickling from one corner. A bruise was coming up on his left eye as well.

He saw me, and fresh tears started from his eyes. I froze, not sure at first what to do. Then I rushed over, leaning down and laying my hand on his shoulder. "You okay, man?"

He shook his head, his lips trembled. "No." He paused; his eyes locked with mine. "I'm gonna kill him." He whispered fiercely.

"No." I shook my head firmly. "No, man. It ain't worth it. You ain't gonna do nothin' foolish. Here, let's get you cleaned up." I gripped his upper arm and pulled him to his feet, turning him to the washstands on the wall outside the shower. I turned on the cold water and said, "Let me go tell Coach something. I'll be right back."

I ran back out of the locker and saw the class in full practice running basketball drills on the court. Coach was on the far side but caught my eye as I stepped out the locker. He raised his eyebrows and cocked his head at me. I waved my hand and then stuck up two fingers to indicate just another minute or two. He shrugged and turned to holler at another boy, "Sloppy pass! That was sloppy, Tirone! Do it again! And do it right this time!"

I went back into the locker and found that Trent had wiped his face with wet paper towels and was drying it now, tenderly laying the dry cloth across the abraded areas. He was going to have a shiner and his lips were going to be tender and bruised for a while too. There was nothing to do about it but go out and act like nothing was wrong.

"Don't be thinking anything foolish, Trent." I said again, urgently.

He looked back at me in the mirror over the sink and I was shocked by the changes in his face. He was suddenly older. He didn't say anything, just looked at me, and then turned and left the locker room without saying another word.

We fell into drills, but I saw Coach talking to Trent on the side a while later. Trent was just standing there, shaking his head, not saying anything. Coach would say something, and Trent would just shake his head, looking off somewhere over the basketball hoop in the upper corner of the high ceiling. Eventually Coach gave up, throwing up his hands and Trent headed for the locker room. I looked around quickly, but Cody and Ronnie were busy doing passing drills.

I didn't see Trent the rest of that day. He must have skipped out. He wasn't at lunch and I didn't see him when I walked home that afternoon. I considered stopping by his apartment to check on him, but I wasn't sure if he was even there, or if he'd spent the day hanging out somewhere, so his mom wouldn't know he'd missed school. I wondered how he would explain his bruises.

The next morning when I came out of the building to head to school, hunching my shoulders against the cold wind blowing hard out of the north, I almost ran into Trent. One minute I was alone in the faint early morning light, arc sodium lights glowing eerily in that last hour before the sun overpowers them and they wink out, and then the next minute I'm almost bowling him over, my left arm and shoulder hitting him hard. He lurched, and I almost slipped on a thin patch of ice on the cracked sidewalk. "Hey!" I cried out, clutching my homework and books as they started to slide out of my arms.

"Hey yourself!" He replied tersely, catching his own balance.

I looked at him then and wasn't surprised to see the black eye or the bruises around the corner of his mouth. The lower lip looked split and raw. He met my gaze steadily for a moment and then looked away, a grim set to his mouth.

"You all right?" I asked, not sure what to say, wanting to know what had happened, wanting to know what he was thinking.

He gave a little shrug with the shoulder nearest me. "Yeah."

We walked some more in silence, breath condensing and leaving a stream as we passed, like little airplane trails behind us. "What happened?" I finally asked.

At first, I wasn't sure Trent had heard. I had spoken softly but I thought loudly enough. There were the usual early morning sounds of a city waking up, commuters heading to jobs just as we were heading to our job of learning, but it wasn't unusually noisy. I turned an inquiring look towards Trent and was about to ask the question again when he finally answered. "I don't want to talk about it."

"Oh." I felt curiously deflated. I hadn't expected him to refuse to tell me. I thought we shared everything. Apparently, there were limits.

We continued to school without saying anything more. He was quiet when I saw him, trying to keep a low profile and not draw any attention. When we met for lunch, I saw he'd brought a sack with a sandwich, some chips and a pudding cup. He grabbed a table near the door while I went through the line to get my lunch. As I slid into the seat across from him he said, "My dad was real pissed when he saw me last night."

I paused in the act of opening my milk carton and looked at him again, harder.

He felt my gaze and met my eyes. "No. None that you can see, anyway."

We both knew what he was talking about. Trent didn't have the best relationship with his dad. I'd learned through the years and from exposure that Trent's dad was a roughneck and he was sorely disappointed in his offspring. He doted on Trent's little sister, Erin, which made his rejection of Trent even more painful.

"He was late. I thought maybe I'd even get off to bed before he got home

120

but that didn't work out." Trent's voice was bitter. I knew that getting home late usually also meant getting home drunk.

I pushed the mushy pasta the school called spaghetti around on the tray, using my bread to push the soggy strands onto the fork, gray bits of what I hoped were ground meat clinging to the red paste the pasta was slathered with. "Was it bad?" I asked softly.

"Not really. He pushed me around a bit. Asked why I let them push me around at school. Did a lot of hollering. Mom cried."

I knew that hurt Trent most of all. I suspected Trent's mom knew he had it hard in school and she knew more than anyone how hard he had it at home. She tried to compensate for it and he idolized her because of it.

Then, for a moment, he was the Trent I was more familiar with. His eyes brightened, and he flashed me a grin. "Hey, why don't you come over tomorrow? See if your mom'll let you come over for the day. There's somethin' I want to do. Come over at about nine."

"Okay, sure!" I knew we didn't have anything going on and there was no reason my mom wouldn't agree.

I was at Trent's the next morning at nine as we'd agreed. Trent's mom opened the door and I entered a world of heavenly smells. One of the advantages of being Trent's friend was Trent's mom. I inhaled deeply and turned wondering eyes towards her.

She smiled warmly. "Red velvet cupcakes," she answered my unspoken question, "And they'll be ready for consumption when you and Trent get back."

She turned and headed back into her kitchen and I followed like a lemming towards that wonderful scent. Trent's mom kept their apartment neat and clean considering the two children and their assorted toys in such cramped quarters. The kitchen looked freshly cleaned now and I saw two pans of dark red cupcakes cooling on the counter. These were one of my favorites! She'd fill them with a cream cheese icing and spread more on top when they'd cooled. My mouth watered at the sight of them.

Trent came bounding through the kitchen doorway. "Hey, you ready?"

"Trent!" his mother exclaimed, "Is that how you say good morning?"

He froze, face slumping into that expression that read Really? while not daring to verbalize. Then he looked at me woodenly and said, "'Mornin'."

I heard his mom sigh deeply and resignedly, knowing she'd get no more from him, as she turned back to pull out a stick of butter and pack of cream cheese. While she was busy moving these to the counter Trent grabbed my arm and pulled me out of the kitchen into the adjoining living room. Erin, six years old, was sitting cross legged on the couch, eating dry cereal out of a bowl and watching cartoons. "Let's go!" Trent said urgently, pulling me to the door. "Be back this afternoon, mom!" He called loudly, as he opened the door to the apartment.

"Okay." Her voice floated back over the smells of freshly baked cupcakes. I followed Trent reluctantly into the grimy hallway. It was true the hallway was grimy, but it always seemed much grimier somehow after being in Trent's apartment. Not that my mom didn't keep ours tidy. She did…just not as tidy as Trent's mom.

We headed out of the building, Trent not divulging our destination. We headed south, away from the cluster of tenement buildings in the industrial, southeastern part of the city and edged to the southwest, into the now mostly derelict former manufacturing section. At one time, maybe two decades ago, this part of the city had been a thriving location with factories of all different types employing thousands of people. Now, it was largely deserted. Tall, razor-wire edged fences blocked off whole blocks with massive dead-eyed buildings lurking. It almost felt as if the wire were protecting them from the buildings, rather than keeping them out.

Trent squatted next to the corner section of one of these fenced buildings and I saw that the fence had been cut from the bottom to about three feet up. He pulled back on this section now and motioned me to go through. I looked around nervously but there was no one in sight. All of these buildings on this block were abandoned and this street offered no handy shortcut to any passing traffic. Quickly, I hunched down and crawled through the opening on my hands and knees, Trent following closely behind.

Once on the other side of the fence, Trent stood up, looked around to make sure we were still unobserved and then ran to the nearest corner of the looming brick edifice and disappeared around the dark corner that formed an alley with the hulking structure next door, the fence between the two buildings further narrowing the alley. I followed Trent, my heart thumping excitedly.

The alley was vaguely threatening, dark, with little of the morning light reaching into the dark tunnel. As we progressed further, passing a hulking trash bin sitting aslant as though the building had tried to shrug it off at some point in the past, it got darker and colder. Then Trent stopped, and I ran into his back.

"Hey!" He whispered urgently, a touch of anger present, again…a change. The old Trent would have laughed where the new Trent became irritated over little things like a bump in a dark alley.

He had stopped at a window and I saw that the pane was empty, no glass reflecting the weak light filtering down. Trent hoisted himself up and over the windowsill, dropping lightly to the floor inside. He turned and reached out a hand, offering me help as I clambered over behind him. Once in we stood for a moment, looking around. It was hard to see but I could sense the immensity of the space before us. Overhead I heard the far away rustle of wings and I wondered uneasily what manner of bird would choose to roost in such a dim and dark space.

Trent moved forward away from me, crossing the space assuredly and I sensed he'd been here before. He looked over his shoulder at me now and said, "Come on!"

I followed, gazing about at the huge interior of the building. It was mostly just a husk of a shell, there was little to no interior structure. Just one large room that seemed to stretch away forever. It was an optical illusion, of course, as the space was not infinite. The building was about fifty feet long and another sixty wide and was probably three stories tall. I saw as we moved away from the window that there was a second and third story built over the second half of the structure on one side of the building and the other half was open the entire three stories. A service elevator ran up along one wall.

"Used to make clothes here." Trent announced; his voice unnaturally loud in the unbroken silence.

I flinched from the sound, not wanting to disturb the stillness. Growing up in a busy city, living in a tenement and attending a crowded public school, I had little personal experience with stillness or silence. Even the public library had to tolerate the sounds of a city outside its doors: horns honking, exhaust systems rumbling, the general turmoil a person becomes immune to but instantly identifies an absence of. The absence made me feel uneasy.

My unease increased when I saw what Trent held in his hand, the gleaming barrel reflecting what little light there was. The next instant my heart lurched a bit and I felt a surge of excited adrenalin. "Trent!" I exclaimed and looked at him questioningly.

"I want to shoot it." He said it as a matter of fact, like it was no big deal.

I looked around wildly. "Here?"

"Sure. Why not? Whose gonna see us?"

It was true. No one knew we were here, and it was unlikely anyone would hear the shots in this mostly deserted section of the city.

Something clicked in my head, and I looked at Trent again, afraid suddenly. "Trent. You're not thinking of…you know…of doing anything…" I didn't know how to continue, but images of those pages I'd seen appeared in my memory.

Trent looked at me quizzically. "Whatcha' mean?"

"I don't know." I shrugged, suddenly embarrassed to have suspected Trent yet not able to squelch the feeling. I moved uneasily back towards the open window and Trent stepped with me, holding out his hand.

"No, man. Go on…say it." He said, his voice low and fierce.

I swallowed past the sudden lump in my throat, aware of the gun in Trent's hand and aware of his propensity to anger. Nervously, I pressed forward. "The school shootings. You weren't doin' research for Social Studies." It came out accusingly and I realized my hands were clenched into fists at my sides, ready to defend myself. I tried to relax, not succeeding.

And then Trent laughed. I felt insulted and the stew of adrenalin became a nauseating mass in my stomach. "Don't laugh at me!" I responded angrily.

Which only made Trent laugh more. Then he stopped, the laugh trickling into a chuckle. "You thought I was gonna shoot up the school!" He chuckled again and turned away from me, fiddling with the gun. "Nah." He said it conversationally as he held the gun out fully extended and sighted along his right arm. Then he lowered it and looked back at me. "No. I wanted to know the outcomes. Not what those kids did but what happened after."

That didn't make sense to me. "If you weren't planning to do it, why does it matter?"

He shrugged. "I guess it doesn't. Most of 'em died anyway. Usually self-inflicted. There's a couple in prison...most of 'em classified as mental."

He turned away and again lifted his arm and sighted along the barrel slowly swinging the barrel along the opposite wall before lowering his arm again.

"I still don't get it." I couldn't help but say it. I didn't get it. If he wasn't planning something, then why were we here doing this?

He sighed, his expression similar to the one I saw him use when he was explaining something to Erin, and I felt resentment that he was treating me that way. Patiently, he explained. "I'm gonna defend myself. I ain't gonna let Keith nor anyone else push me around anymore. So, I need to know how to use this."

Clearly the plan made perfect sense to Trent. I wasn't as convinced. "I don't know, man. You gonna carry that around in school?"

"If I have to." His voice took on a tone of belligerence.

"I don't think that's cool."

"I don't care what you think." Voice brutal now.

I shrugged. "So, what now?"

"So, now I shoot the gun. Why don't you stand back behind me?"

I shrugged again, feeling resentful and afraid. We were about twenty feet from the far wall, standing near a pillar supporting a second-floor beam close to the center of the building. I leaned against the pillar off to Trent's right and about five feet behind him while he assumed the stance we'd seen on all the cop shows: feet spread about shoulder length apart, right arm locked straight out with gun extended, left hand bracing his right wrist. He swiveled slowly and then froze. "See that paint mark on the wall over there?"

I peered through the gloom at the far wall and saw a gleam of white on one of the cinderblocks about four feet off the floor. "Yeah. You mean that white smear?"

He nodded. "Yeah. That's what I'm aimin' at."

The explosion in the cavernous space was deafening. I clapped my hands to my unprotected ears and felt something like a punch in my lower right abdomen. Seconds later I heard a clatter as Trent dropped the gun and it crashed on the concrete floor, spinning away from us, the barrel turning in a hazardous arc before coming to rest pointing across the floor away from us. Slowly, I sank to my knees.

I peered down at my stomach and the growing stain of red with disbelief and I suddenly felt very faint and very cold. I pressed my hands to the spot and looked up at Trent in terror.

His eyes were wide in shock and all color was draining from his face. "Oh, shit, man." And then he rushed to me, falling to his knees in front of me. "Man, man, man. It's okay. Gonna get you some help. Okay?"

I nodded, not fully comprehending what had happened but not able to refute the terrible pain that was spreading now from my guts. I needed to lie down; I couldn't hold myself up. I slumped to the side and Trent helped keep my head from hitting the concrete. He helped me stretch out on my left side and pressed my hands into my right side. "Keep pressure." He said urgently. "I've got to go for help. I don't want to leave you but I gotta. You gotta keep pressure. Okay?"

I nodded, unable to speak. I felt curiously removed from the situation, numb. I wanted to sleep, and I closed my eyes. Just a short nap. Maybe if I dozed.

Then, Trent was shaking my shoulder urgently. "No, man! Wake up! Come on! You gotta stay alert, gotta keep pressure. I gotta get help!"

I could hear the panic in his voice, and I responded, struggling against the lethargy, nodding weakly. "Go!" I managed to force out.

I don't remember much after that, and I didn't remember that much at first. I was in intensive care for two weeks and had two major surgeries. The bullet, which had ricocheted off the cinderblock wall, nicked my right kidney and came within inches of my spine. They tried to save my kidney with the first surgery but that failed. The second surgery was to remove the failing organ. We hoped for a donor kidney but to this day I have just the one kidney.

Trent and I remained friends through the rest of school. The police, of course, took the gun, and Trent never got another one. It was ruled an accident and he had to attend juvenile parole for the remainder of his teen years, but he did so without one word of complaint that I know of. I know he had to pay restitution though I never saw a cent of it so I'm not sure what Victims Funds are all about. I suppose that's how they paid for my medical care and surgeries.

Trent and I drifted apart after school, which seems to be normal. I'm an IT tech guy at the local hospital where I do all right. I've got a wife, two kids and a hefty mortgage. I'm careful about my one kidney.

Trent went on to be a successful author. I read his author's bio on Amazon and wasn't surprised there was no mention of his childhood or his friend. Why would there be? That's not the sort of thing you read in an author's bio. Still, I think the events of that day may have prevented a disaster of greater proportions. I think Trent was on the path to becoming a mass school shooter. I believe he was on the border of some line that relentless bullying would have forced him to cross eventually.

I learned later that Trent ran to the nearest person he could flag down which just happened to be a cruising police officer. The officer followed Trent back to the abandoned factory and rendered assistance, calling in additional help and an ambulance, before taking Trent into custody. My parents wanted to press charges, but I begged them not to. Eventually they agreed but Trent was never a welcome guest in our apartment after that. I never did get my red velvet cupcake that day, but a dozen of them showed up at the hospital. I smile at that thought now. It was almost worth a bullet to get a dozen red velvet cupcakes all my own!

ABOUT THE AUTHOR

Cheryl King is an author who lives in Eureka Springs, Arkansas with her lifetime partner and best friend, her husband Harland. She is the author of *Corpocracy*, a novel.

The story 'Red Sky at Dawn' from this collection was chosen for inclusion in the 2019 edition of eMerge Magazine, the online magazine of the Writers' Colony at Dairy Hollow in Eureka Springs.

www.ingramcontent.com/pod-product-compliance
Lightning Source LLC
Chambersburg PA
CBHW020408130626
46549CB00006B/2480